D1523433

THE
PANGERSBOURNE
MURDERS

Also by J.G. Jeffreys

The Village of Rogues
A Wicked Way to Die
The Wilful Lady
A Conspiracy of Poisons
Suicide Most Foul
Captain Bolton's Corpse

THE
PANGERSBOURNE
MURDERS

by
J.G. Jeffreys

Walker and Company ✸ New York

190

First published in the United States of America in 1984 by the Walker
Publishing Company, Inc.

ISBN: 0-8027-5572-0

Library of Congress Catalog Card Number: 83-42728

Printed in the United States of America

10 9 8 7 6 5 4 3 2

EDITOR'S NOTE

As usual Mr Sturrock uses a great many fictitious names; presumably, as he explains elsewhere, to avoid what he calls "embarrassment". Hence Wittings End and Milton Pangersbourne are unknown in Hampshire and the New Forest today, and there is no official record of the extraordinary cricket match played on the latter village green on Saturday August 26, 1815. Neither have I been able to find any mention of a "Dr Wilford Caldwell" in the formidable list of American explorers and botanists of the early 19th century.

On the other hand Sturrock's references to both cricket and horticulture are absolutely factual. As a follower of the Marylebone Club his knowledge of cricket is not surprising, but it seems quite clear that horticulture was completely outside his experience. His references to it therefore can only suggest that he must have been working with someone who had a wide knowledge of that field, and of the numerous American plants which were being introduced to England at this time.

The traffic in fact had started from Virginia with the Tradescant family as early as the first half of the 17th century, and by the 19th it was reaching its peak.

America then was regarded as a treasure land of new and sometimes very strange plants, and so far from being "eccentric"—as Sturrock describes him—the unfortunate Lord Pangersbourne was merely following the fashion of innumerable other English country gentlemen in collecting them. Nor is it unlikely that the curious little specimen, which was indirectly responsible for his death, could have aroused something like terror in Milton Pangersbourne, since the villagers there would certainly have never seen or heard of anything like it before.

B.J.H.

ONE

It is a matter of fact that a woman in a bachelor establishment, even one of only thirteen years, is like a sharp end of horsehair in the seat of a man's chair; a discomfort where he least welcomes it. Upon which observation I shall now present a teasing little private mystery of a more domestic sort than my usual more important business as the first officer and ornament of the Bow Street Police Force. In short the mystery of the calamity child known as Peggoty—or more precisely Miss Amelia Lydia Clarissa Pangersbourne—discovered in the wicked cellars of Wapping, and rescued at extreme danger to ourselves by me and Master Maggsy.*

A child of misfortune, being the fruit of a clandestine marriage between an actress unknown and one Roderick, only son of a certain Lord Pangersbourne; who refused to recognise the marriage, if it ever existed. Whereupon this mysterious young lady first caused the baby to be delivered to the old lord in a theatrical hamper, with her compliments, and then took herself off, while Roderick also disappeared; all this about 1802. Thereafter nothing was ever heard of the woman

* *Captain Bolton's Corpse*

again, and no more of Roderick either until some seven years later, when he was reported killed during the fearful retreat to Corunna, in Spain, under Sir John Moore in 1809.

Thus the child was brought up by Lord Pangersbourne; as poor as a church flea and twice as eccentric, and a noted botanist and horticulturist, who was struck down by an apoplexy in 1814; said to be consequent on a gardener's letting one of his curious vegetables die for want of water. She was then at the age of twelve and his late lordship was declared insolvent; and being threatened with an orphan's home by the village parson she then ran away with a band of gipsies and so found her way to Wapping near London.

So there you have her story—or such of it as we could put together from her various tales—and the common report in London concerning Lord Pangersbourne's death. What follows is the truth of the matter. What we discovered—myself, Dr Wilford Caldwell, my clerk Maggsy and my sporting coachman Jagger—when we set out to investigate, more than twelve months after that unfortunate event. It is a nice example of the difference between common report and truth.

I shall confess that I saw no particular mystery to start with. What moved me was more a consideration for the future peace and quiet of my gentleman's chambers in Soho Square. In short she was an awkward blessing to have about the place, being of an appearance not unlike a pug-dog in repose, as inquisitive as a cat, as talkative as a jay and showing signs of entering into an unholy alliance with the aforesaid Maggsy and Jagger; though a sweet and affectionate child otherwise.

Yet having found the creature we could not abandon her to the streets again, for that would be to put her straight on the primrose path to the Haymarket whore-shops. To return her to Wapping after the affair of the smugglers could well result in getting her throat cut. My dear good friend, Lady Dorothea Hookham-Dashwood, who might have found a modest place for her in some respectable establishment, was presently travelling in Italy and not expected to return for some months to come. And I could not put her out to any of the several somewhat less noble ladies of my acquaintance since, however wide and liberal were their other accomplishments, they could hardly be reckoned precisely suitable as duennas. She had already picked up quite enough ideas in Wapping.

So there was nothing for it but to take leave of absence from my more important duties at Bow Street and find out if there was any of the child's family left to claim her. And uncommonly curious the business turned out to be.

It was clear that I had two lines of inquiry; one that the late Lord Pangersbourne had been a botanist and horti-culturist and the other that the child's mother, name unknown, was an actress. And here our most excellent old Clerk of the Court at Bow Street, Abel Makepenny, was of inestimable worth with the first, for he is a walking directory of the nobility and landed gentry and their pleasures and pursuits, respectable or various.

"Why, Jer'my," said he, dusting the snuff out of his nose when I put the question, "it's as plain as a pike-staff. If your man was a horticulturist it's a guinea to a pinch of bacca that he'll have been a member of the Horticultural Society. And I fancy I see somewhere that there's a meeting this very Saturday." He turned to rustling over the sheets of *The Times* newspaper, muttering, "This demned snuff, I'll swear they put pepper in it nowadays," and then announcing: "Here

9

we have it. 'Today's Arrangements. The Horticultural Society, eleven o'clock forenoon at Hatchard's Bookshop, Piccadilly. Dr Wilford Caldwell. Some observations on Recent Travels on the Orinoco and Demerara Rivers'."

"Hold now," I commanded. "Dr Wilford Caldwell? That name chimes with me somewhere. Now where was that? One of my cases, I wonder, some years back?"

Abel shook his head. "I take leave to doubt it. These ain't the sort of gentry to touch any Bow Street affair. Demnition respectable. The Right Honourable Charles Greville and the Right Honourable Sir Joseph Banks. He's the one that sailed to the South Seas with Captain Cook, and named Botany Bay. Must be getting on in his seventies now, and a touch of the martinet they say. You'll have to mind your manners in that company."

"I mind my manners in any company," I retorted as I took my leave.

So giving Jagger his orders we turned the chaise westwards, with Master Maggsy and Miss Peggoty riding with me; the one looking near enough like a young gentleman, except for his wicked face, and the other the picture of demurity in a pretty sprigged gown and little bonnet chosen for her by one of my ladies, who has a nice genteel taste in such matters if somewhat more open-minded in others. It was a sunshiny day of August in the year 1815, and an animated scene in Piccadilly. Ladies in their muslins, ribbons and parasols, gentlemen taking the air and riders trotting up towards the Green Park, urchins raising a cheer every time they caught sight of a soldier—although most of the Army was still in occupation of Paris—and a spanking array of

10

carriages; my own turnout and cattle not the least smart of any of 'em. No bumping or cursing, for a miracle, all in a cheerful humour for our recent victories, Bonaparte now on his way to where he couldn't do any more mischief, and nobody yet starting to count the cost.

Nevertheless I was more concerned with Dr Wilford Caldwell than the lively spectacle and the chatter of Peggoty and Master Maggsy, as it vexes me exceedingly when I cannot put a name I know to its occasion. But then Providence Himself came to my aid, as He always does with those who attend church on Sundays; for, just as Jagger edged a town phaeton out of the way and got us into the only empty space at the curb by Hatchard's, I perceived the very man himself emerging with a knot of others from the bookshop. As Abel Makepenny had observed, a most respectable company, all frock coats and top hats, exchanging compliments in the politest manner possible, one irascible old gentleman attended by a coachman and valet that I took to be the great Sir Joseph Banks; and the face rough-carved out of teak-wood, the sharp dark eyes and the little goatee beard which brought it all back in a stroke.

The affair that I always thought of as the French spies and the poisoned whore; and she also an actress of a sort. The dreadful resurrection of a corpse by midnight and carrying it back to London through the pouring rain, to Bart's Hospital in the hope of discovering the cause of death; and this eminent American explorer and scientist of Philadelphia who had explained to us the nature of the mysterious Indian poison never before heard of in this country. Not that he had anything to do with these dark events, for he was a most upright and reputable man.*

* *A Conspiracy of Poisons*

11

As I say, I knew him on the instant, nor was Master Maggsy far behind me. "God's Whiskers," he ejaculated, "That's the cove who told us all about the wild Indians and their nasty habits." But the biggest surprise came from Miss Peggoty, for no sooner had Jagger pulled our horses up than she cried, "Why, Uncle Wilford!", scrambled down out of the chaise with a most unseemly display of petticoats and slippers and galloped across to him; and it was just as clear that he recognised her.

It was a scene of some small polite confusion; Dr Caldwell announcing, "Well now, little Amelia Lydia," the great Sir Joseph observing, "Here's a pert, pretty miss," the other gentlemen drawing off with various reminders of dining and supping etc., the doctor bending his gaze on me, saying, "We've met somewhere before, sir," and Peggoty crying, "It's my new Uncle Sturrock."

"Some time since, sir," I reminded him. "You were generous to give me your advice on certain scientific matters. And if I don't interrupt your other occasions I shall be obliged for a few further words now, concerning the late Lord Pangersbourne. My club's no more than a few steps away in St James's Street, and we keep a very fair Solero."

"Pangersbourne, eh?" he asked, glancing down at Miss Peggoty. "Aye: I'd heard that he'd passed on to do his gardening elsewhere, and if there's any way I can be of use you've only to ask. Likewise a glass or two of Madeira will go down nicely after all that talking."

So the matter was amicably arranged; and, having instructed Jagger to take a turn in the Green Park with Maggsy and Peggoty and come back for us in an hour, we went amiably on our way.

As my esteemed readers will know, my more common haunt was The Brown Bear in Drury Lane, and a very suitable place for your ordinary run of cutthroats and villains; but a man must keep in step with his better social obligations and I had lately been elected to this select rendezvous for professional gentlemen by the good offices of our Chief Magistrate at Bow Street. Dr Caldwell was polite enough to approve highly of it, and of our wine there, and once settled in the smoking room with a bottle between us I lost no time about plunging into my tale.

"So there we have it," I concluded. "There's a certain small competence I'm holding for the child, but beyond that she's penniless, and so far as I can make out there's not a soul in the world she can call her own except this actress mother. If the woman's still alive. I shall try to trace the creature as a matter of course, but even if I find her it don't strike me that she's the sort to have the care of a rising young girl."

"Your concern does you credit, sir," Dr Caldwell announced. "But I'll own I'm considerably puzzled. Pangersbourne died insolvent, you tell me?"

"If not worse, on all the information I have."

"Then we've a tarnation odd problem here." He mused over it for a minute and then continued, "See now, Mr Sturrock, I'll start at the beginning as you have with me, and then we'll see what we can make of it all. I first met Pangersbourne some six or seven years back. He was a corresponding member of the American Philosophical Society. That's how I had my introduction, and I've visited with him four, maybe five times. He never mentioned any of his family and it wasn't my place to ask. I gathered that he didn't choose to talk of 'em, if any, so I can't help you much there. But he presented the child as his grand-daughter, and clearly had a fondness for her. And he once told me that all he had would pass on to her. I'd say she should be a very moderate heiress."

"Seemingly to somewhat less than nothing," I observed.

He shook his head. "That's what I don't understand. I'm told he died about a twelvemonth since, and that being so I was with him no more than a few weeks before the event; on the eve of my latest journey to the Orinoco. In short, Mr Sturrock, he subscribed two hundred guineas to the expedition, and offered more if it was needed. That ain't exactly the procedure of a man in insolvency or worse."

"He subscribed two hundred guineas?" I repeated.

The good doctor was a trifle impatient. "It's a common practice among the gentlemen amateurs. Joseph Banks has laid out thousands on such ventures at one time or another. They have the scientific interest, and they look to receive a proportion of any new plants or seeds or other curiosities that may be discovered."

I reflected that I was getting into eccentric waters for a Bow Street man, and he continued, "But that's not the whole of it. When I last saw Pangersbourne he was much engaged with a certain little plant which so far as I'm aware has not yet been cultivated successfully in this country; nor anywhere else for that matter outside its natural surroundings, although not uncommon in the bogs and swamps of Virginia. There's reference to old John Bartram sending specimens over in the last forties or fifties, and it seems that his rival, William Young, sent others a bit later. But there's no record of any of them ever growing."

Since neither of these names meant anything to me, nor could I see what they might possibly have to do with Miss Peggoty's predicament, I could offer little

14

more than a polite interest. Nevertheless I inquired, "Does this have a bearing on the matter we are discussing?"

"It does indeed," he assured me. "You say that Pangersbourne was taken with an apoplexy consequent on one of his plants being allowed to die for want of water; and I've heard much the same, though in somewhat different details, from other gentlemen. And I'd say that this was the plant in question. In short, *Dionaea muscipula*.'

That, however, was too much. You can allow these botanical experts to ride their hobby-horses within reason, but this was the trot too far. "In very short," I observed. "But you have the advantage of me."

He permitted himself a brief smile. "I ask your pardon, Mr Sturrock. We botanists are apt to be a trifle pedantic at times. Venus's Fly Trap; known also in America as the Tippitiwichet. An engaging little beauty of not more than six or eight inches which catches and eats flies. And has a most voracious appetite for 'em too."

I started, "Come, sir," now beginning to grow exceedingly irritated, but he held up his hand, saying, "Hear me out, Mr Sturrock. For unless I'm much mistaken we've a very curious business here. As curious as the plant itself. I've a notion that you've been a mite misled by the simplest explanation, as have other people. The thing couldn't have died for want of water. Pangersbourne was a skilled horticulturalist and so was his plant-house man. They'd have perceived that the plant was dry and taken steps to correct the condition in time. No, sir; I'd say what it died from was the *wrong sort of water*."

"Now, sir," I protested again, "this is growing too profound for me," but he went on regardless, and

15

somewhat grim, "It'll come clear enough. Pangersbourne had received a bare pinch of the seed from another of his correspondents in America. He had tried it by several various methods, and had contrived to raise five seedlings; which was a sufficient achievement, although four of 'em failed in the end. But the last one was a fine, healthy specimen. That I'm sure of, for he showed it me himself in his plant-house." He paused for effect and took the chance to refresh himself. "And here's the nub of the matter, sir. He had laid a wager of no less than five hundred guineas that he would raise one or more of those plants from seed to flower."

"He did what?" I gazed at him in astonishment. "Then the man was more than a mere eccentric. He was clean out of his wits."

"Bigger wagers have been laid on smaller matters before now," Caldwell observed. "Nevertheless I told him much the same thing. We have a name for speaking our minds in Philadelphia. Whereupon I was advised in no uncertain terms to mind my own damned business. But you'll see what I'm coming to. The Fly Trap is a native of the moss bogs. Its only simple need is tempered rain water, although Pangersbourne held that that was better with a knob or two of peat steeped in it. Anything else would be near enough poison. A handful of common lime or soda in the water-butt would be quite enough."

"So ho," I mused, smart on the uptake as I am. "In short, to use a vulgar sporting parlance, you're proposing that this fantastical vegetable was nobbled."

"To use another vulgar sporting parlance, I'm saying it's a racing certainty."

"Then we've got a bone with some meat on it now," I said. "Who was it? Who did Pangersbourne lay this wager with?"

"There's the rub," the doctor announced calmly. "I don't know. I've told you, he instructed me to mind my own damned business, and he was a man of uncommon choleric temperament. Nothing more was said about the matter."

I pondered over that a minute. "It's vexatious. But he had gardeners?"

"He had three. Two men and a boy. The head was in charge of his plant-house; a Thomas Grubbage."

"Then this Grubbage is the one we must look to."

Dr Caldwell shook his head once more. "I doubt it. He struck me as an honest fellow. And the others were never allowed near the plant unless he or Pangersbourne was present. Likewise and again that is not the establishment of a gentleman on the edge of bankruptcy."

"Sir," I assured him earnestly, "you'd be surprised at what our Bow Street clerk, old Abel Makepenny, can tell you about the landed gentry. Even I am now and again; and there's very little surprises me. He could have been up to his snout in debt, and looking to the five hundred guineas to pay off a bit of it."

But the doctor remained firm and adamant about that. "Not Pangersbourne, Mr Sturrock. I'll tell you flat, I don't believe it. He was as frugal in his morals as his style. And there's one more matter, Mr Sturrock, though there's little doubt the lawyers would wine and dine on it for a lifetime if it ever came to the point with the child. He held the title to a considerable tract of land on the Rappahannock River in Virginia; and somewhat proud of it, for on one occasion he showed me the deeds. Maybe you're familiar with the constitution of the ancient Virginia Company?"

To tell the truth I had never so much as heard of it, and I answered cautiously. "The precise details escape

17

my memory."

"I would not have known them myself had not Pangersbourne explained 'em at some length," he confessed kindly. "The Company was formed in 1617, or thereabouts, by a number of travellers and merchant adventurers. They held a charter to issue shares in the sum of twelve pounds ten shillings apiece, and each share entitled the holder to a grant of fifty acres of land." He paused once more and then finished. "Pangersbourne held the title to ten shares, or five hundred acres of land, taken up by an ancestor or forbear of his. Then a plain Isaac Bourne, a wool merchant."

I considered that also, but did not think a lot of it. "1617?" I asked. "Near enough two hundred years back. And you've had your Revolution since then. I'd say the title no longer exists."

"Quite so," he agreed. "I said the lawyers would wine and dine on it for a lifetime. But as I understand, it was the custom then to send out some younger member or dependent of the family to sit on the land. They were among the earliest settlers in Virginia; and few of 'em knew what they were going out to. But that's by the way. I'm proposing merely that it's another matter to reflect on. Especially if you're looking for connections of the family."

"I'll grant you that," I said. "At least it's food for thought."

"In my opinion it's a banquet," he announced, "taken all in all. And if I can assist in any way, pray do not wait to call on me. So if I may be so bold, what are your next intentions?"

"I shall be profoundly grateful for your assistance, sir," I assured him, but privately resolving that I meant to go about the business in my own way. "For my next

18

move I mean to call on a certain theatrical agent of my acquaintance in the hope that he might give us some information about this actress mother; although that is by no means certain. Then of necessity a drive down to this village, Milton Pangersbourne, which I understand is not far from Lyndhurst in the New Forest."

"Far enough," Caldwell said, "and somewhat remote. I recollect that I had the devil of a business to find it when I first went there. But a pretty place; not unlike a village in Virginia. A green and some uncommon fine elms. A smithy, and an inn of sorts, the Pangersbourne Arms; and a water-mill close by. A biggish church for such a place; and, by the way, Pangersbourne was at daggers drawn with the parson over some old matter, a Reverend Athanasius Hangbolt. I never got to the bottom of it, and I never asked; but there was a cricket game one day while I was present, and the two of 'em snarled at each other from a distance like bulldogs. Which reminds me also of the one thing Pangersbourne ever told me about the son, Roderick. That he was a notable young cricketer in his day, and on that account a close friend of the blacksmith. A fellow not improperly named Ironband."

"You paint a picture with the exact eye of Mr Constable," I complimented him. "But very likely a place seething with wickedness under the rural peace, especially if the natives are inclined towards cricket. It's a pursuit that arouses dark passions, though I own to following the Marylebone men myself when I've no more important business on hand. And now, sir," I concluded, "since you've been so good as to offer your assistance, what are your plans?"

He finished the Solera with evident appreciation. "I aim to be here for near enough a month, and I'm engaged to dine or sup with some of the gentlemen of

19

the Horticultural Society, and visit for a day or two with several more; not forgetting the important Sir Joseph Banks. But I've a notion that I might travel down to Milton Pangersbourne myself as soon as may be. In the meantime any message to my lodging, at Mrs Dobie's in Queen Street by the British Museum, will reach me."

"I shall make a particular note of it," I assured him. "And now I perceive my clerk has come to tell us that my chaise has arrived. If you have no more important occasion I propose an adjournment to Hacket's Eating House off Oxford Street. A modest establishment, but we shall be well served, and doubtless Miss Peggoty will delight in telling you an account of her mysterious adventures over the last twelvemonth. Or, as I suppose we must now call the child, Miss Amelia Lydia Clarissa."

After this polite discourse and our following dinner it was latish in the afternoon before we went our several ways; and seeing this was a Saturday I left my call on Mr Sims, the actors' agent, until Monday in the forenoon. This agency was a dark little den above the Harp Tavern in Russell Street, also a dark little place, much decorated with ancient play-bills, broadsheets, Newgate notices, etc., and mostly frequented by just as ancient actors rehearsing past triumphs and future hopes. Mr Sims, however, was highly regarded in the profession as being moderately honest, while I was known to him as being an informed critic of the drama, and had once before asked his advice and assistance in the before mentioned matter of the whore and the mysterious poison.

In person he was a smallish, fattish, roundish man, of a benevolent manner tempered with caution in case you should ask him for something. Like all of these agents, theatrical and otherwise, he was all delight to see you but hoping to God you wouldn't stay too long, but he greeted me kindly enough with the same speech that I swear he always made to all the actors who ever went to him for a part.

"Well it's a pleasure to see you again, Mr Sturrock. You look fine and flourishing. I wish I could say the same about myself, for things are bad; damme I've never known worse. Managements at their wits' end if they ever had any to get to the end of, costs going up, and audiences down, and who can blame 'em with the plays on in London now? With Siddons retired and poor Dick Sheridan declining in his mind there's nothing I'd recommend an organ-grinder's ape to go and see." He paused for breath and surveyed me anxiously. "I suppose you ain't wrote a play or anything silly like that, have you? You'd be surprised at the people who do. Because I'm bound to advise you . . ."

"I have not," I told him firmly. "I'm here on proper business, Mr Sims. But we'll send your clerk Lancelot down to The Harp for a bottle of claret before we come to it." So when that was arranged and the good fellow's anxieties somewhat eased, I announced, "It's a pretty problem, and precious little I can offer you to go on. But it concerns a poor, innocent child who I suspect has been robbed of her inheritance. In short I'm looking for an actress, some thirteen or fourteen years ago, who married one of the landed gentry . . ."

"Oh, begod," he interjected, "damn near all of 'em come into the profession with that one notion glinting in their eyes."

". . . or just as likely didn't marry him," I continued, "but gave birth to a daughter about 1802. The father presumably being a certain Roderick Pangersbourne. But all I can tell you about the woman is that her

21

forename might have been either Amelia, Lydia or Clarissa."

I stopped myself on that, for Mr Sims had heaved his snout out of the pot of claret and was gazing at me over it with his jaw damned nearly dropping off. "Well I'll be be—," he observed, next bawled "Lancelot!" and then, when that youth poked his head out of his own little den, demanded, "Tell Mr Sturrock about the gent who was here last Friday. Captain the Honourable what the Devil was it?

I fancy this Lancelot was a child of the Hebraic fraternity, but otherwise not unlike Maggsy save for a pimple or two; just as sharp, though not quite so wicked. "Captain the Hon. Wilberforce Haggard," he said. "I wrote it down."

"And asked pretty well the same as you," added Mr Sims. "Whereupon I told him it was out of all hope and reason, and it'd take a month of Sundays to search the books, but if he liked to make it worth his while my clerk might do the job."

"Which I done," Master Lancelot said. "Took all day the Saturday. Found her in 1801 and 1802. Miss Clarissa du Frésne de Champillion. Aged seventeen. Sweet and winsome maiden parts."

"Uncommon sweet and winsome," I observed feelingly. "Was that her real name?"

"For God's sake whoever heard of a name like Clarissa du Frésne de Champillion?" Mr Sims demanded. "She was most likely plain Euphonia Trumpetblower, or something of the sort."

"Working the Western Tour, Guildford, Winchester, Southampton, Salisbury," the clerk recited. "And so on with one-nighters in-between. *Rivals, Duenna, Trip to Scarborough, School for Scandal.*"

"So did you give him that information?" I asked.

22

"And did he make it worth your while?"

"Wouldn't have got it nohow if he hadn't," Master Lancelot answered, thus confirming my notion of his paternity. "Had to take it to him at the Belle Sauvage, and I says 'It's five of the best for the search fee, your Honourable; or I don't know nothing and ain't like to find out'. And Mr Sims copped for half of that anyway."

"You're a sharp fellow," I told him. "You'll go far. But what style of man was he? Age? Appearance? Was he an actor or a gentleman?"

"Can't hardly tell one from t'other, can you?" the dreadful youth inquired reasonably. "Got a cavalry cut about him; leastways cavalry mustachios. You might say thirty to fortyish. Kind of yellerish, brownish, leathery colour; and might be a bit of a roarer if he tried. Put me in mind of a cove we had who played *Mazeppa and the Wild Horse*, and *Turpin's Ride to York*." He appealed to Mr Sims. "The one that broke his neck at the Garden the night his horse took fright and jumped over the footlights at the catcalls and orange peel from the gallery."

"I recollect the rascal," Mr Sims announced. "He died owing me money; and never could ride anyhow. Well now, Mr Sturrock," he added, finishing the claret, "It's a pleasure to have been of service to you, but if there's nothing else I'm appointed to wait on Mr Arnold at the Drury Lane by one o'clock."

"And I'm obliged to you," I assured him. "But there's one matter more. What was this woman's real name? For I'll take my oath it wasn't Euphonia Trumpetblower."

Mr Sims looked at Lancelot again, and the child of Moses gazed at the ceiling. There was no doubt that having sniffed money once he was running to the scent again. "I dunno that I just recollect," he mused. "It was

23

something uncommon common. Would it be worth five guineas?"

"Come now, my lad," I told him sharpish. "Let's have no nonsense. If I find a crime's been committed, as I think it has, and you're withholding information, you'll find yourself giving it at Bow Street. I'll have the woman's proper name and all else you know about her."

There are few dare resist me when I take that tone. Mr Sims advised, "You best speak up, Lancelot, for he's a wicked man when he's crossed," and the money-grubbing little wretch confessed sulkily "Clara Comfrey."

"Begod we're getting a plenitude of riches now," I observed. "And what else?"

"There ain't nothing else," Mr Sims said. "For God's sake, it was thirteen years or more ago. So far as I can recollect business was bad, and the company broke up somewhere about Salisbury."

"Did you ever hear any more of her after that?"

"Never a word," he declared. "And never wanted to."

"Until this Captain the Honourable Wilberforce Haggard comes inquiring," I mused. "And that's what you told him?" I asked Lancelot. "So what did *he* say?"

"Nothing; or not a lot," the clerk said unwillingly. "Claimed it wasn't much for his money, and wanted to know . . ."

He stopped short there and I finished for him, "He wanted to know the names of the other actors and actresses in the company, and the management. And so do I." I held up my hand to stem further protest. "Not on this instant. I'll not keep you from your proper business any longer, Mr Sims. But it will be worth half a guinea to your boy if he likes to write it all down and leave it for me at The Brown Bear at some convenient

24

time today."

"Mr Sturrock," Mr Sims announced with feeling, "your open-handed generosity is the talk of the clubs and coffee-houses."

"And justly so," I said as I took my leave.

This was the Monday and little more to report of that day, save that I despatched Jagger to the Belle Sauvage to make certain inquiries, for a sporting coachman can often learn wonders from ostlers and stable-lads. I was exceedingly inquisitive about this Honourable Haggard and why he should have started questions much the same as mine, and made a point to ask old Abel Makepenny whether he had ever heard of the family. But neither brought much to light. Abel said, "Begod, there's dozens of Haggards; though I never heard of an Honourable among 'em," while all Jagger discovered was that the said gentleman had looked a likely cove but was careful with his money, and had left by the Salisbury coach the Sunday morning—that being yesterday—in company with a lady. In short it was suspicious, and an oddity but so far nothing more.

Neither did the further information from Mr Sims's office amount to very much for the expenditure of half a guinea. It was a brief note announcing, "The best we can do, and God knows what's happened to this lot by now, but the three marked are known to be dead either by booze, debt or other misfortune," and a much frayed and discoloured play-bill, plainly of a poorish sort. "Presenting a DISTINGUISHED COMPANY of the MOST CELEBRATED LADIES AND GENTLE-MEN,' it said, 'from the THEATRES ROYAL, DRURY LANE AND HAYMARKET, LONDON, in a Season of Plays by MR RICHARD SHERIDAN, under the personal management and direction of MR

R. W. ELLISTON.' Thereafter followed a list of some eight or ten names, two men and a woman being crossed through, and Miss Clarissa du Frésne de Champillion only third from the bottom. "So she didn't amount to much," I observed. "And no more does this, but we'll keep it by us in case it might be useful."

We were then sitting over our Madeira and pipes, myself, Master Maggsy and Jagger, who had just delivered his report on the Belle Sauvage and Captain the Honourable. Miss Amelia Lydia had been packed off to her bed all agog at the thought of driving back to Milton Pangersbourne in our spanking style—though for discretion's sake not yet told very much otherwise—Maggsy was philosophising about the oddities of horti-culturists in general and the late Lord Pangersbourne in particular, and wondering in his poetic way whether a mysterious vegetable that eats flies ever gets the belly-ache; and I was delivering my final instructions. "In particular, nothing said in front of Miss Calamity," I ordered. "We don't want everybody told what we're going for, and what she don't hear she can't talk about."

"Won't make a lot of odds if she does," Maggsy observed. "You know what these country savages are: as suspicious as cats. You won't gammon that lot that you've just come to have a dish of tea with the parson in the vestry. And anyway you'll stir up mischief as soon as we get there; you always do." He addressed himself to Jagger. "I reckon we'd best put the pistols in the chaise with the other baggage, Jaggs. What with Sturrock running wild in the country again, and people nobbling these damnation rummy vegetables, I reckon we might need 'em. Maybe we should take a spade as well in case he takes a fancy to dig up another corpse or two."

"Hold your nonsensical chatter," I told the obstre-perous wretch. "It'll be a mere peaceful few days in the sweet country air, observing the beauties of nature and the simple villagers about their innocent pursuits; and maybe even a cricket match on the green."

"That's right," he said darkly. "That's what we're afraid of, me and Jaggs."

TWO

So with that much made clear—and, as no doubt my brass-faced publisher will declare, a deal of chatter to a pennyworth of meat—you may next observe us off to an early start by six o'clock in the morning, by way of Hyde Park Corner and Knightsbridge and taking the turnpike to Hounslow. Once out of the stink of London it was a sweet and balmy day of late August with the mist still rising from the meadows, not a lot on the road after we had left the market carts behind, Jagger carolling a song or two to the lively clip of our cattle, Maggsy and Miss Amelia Lydia chattering like a pair of jays as every fresh prospect unfolded, and myself in reflective and benevolent mood.

All going well, and so far no trouble with mail-coach drivers or other dangers of the highway, we paused to break our fast at The George in Hounslow—a most excellent inn, and a pound or so of steak etc.—where I entertained Miss Amelia with reminiscences of highwaymen on the notorious Heath; though not now so bad as it was at one time, mostly owing to me and others of the Bow Street Force. This brought us to the main part of our journey, a matter of near enough another eighty miles, which Jagger vowed he would do in under the

28

twelve hours from Soho Square to Lyndhurst; and might have tried it, the reckless villain, had I not over-ruled him. Captain the Honourable had two days start on us and there was little point in running our cattle into the ground or going arse over tip into the ditch to try and catch up with him now.

Nevertheless I had Jagger and Maggsy make inquiries at the various other inns we stopped at: The Crown in Staines to relieve ourselves and give the horses a blow, then at several other places of no particular note, and after these The Lion at Blackwater for dinner: where we was presented with the toughest old duck I have ever encountered, choicely stuffed with gallstones. Such are the mischances of travel in these times; and, if that were not enough, when we came out onto the straight stretch known as Hartford Bridge Flats—reputed to be the fastest five miles of coach road in all England—Jagger must needs let his cattle out and essay a trial with a vicious young devil driving a racing curricle. We must have been roaring along at damned near twelve miles an hour, and what with that con-founded duck and the yells and curses, Maggsy's cat-calls, exchanges of whips, etc., Amelia Lydia's screeches and the rocking and wheel-grinding, I finished up with a fit of the farts and rumbles which lasted me all the way to Whitchurch. And here I firmly damned the rude merriment of Master Maggsy and Amelia Lydia and called a halt for the night.

But even a touch of the rumbles may sometimes reveal itself as the Hand of Providence, for we dis-covered The White Hart there to be a commodious inn and a changing-post for several of the coach routes, having a good table, and a brandy of singular excel-lence. With that and a venison pasty, a fine ripe Stilton, a pot or two of claret and the company of several other travellers I was soon restored to my habitual benevolent humour. Whereupon the aforesaid Hand of P. etc., was further manifested when Master Maggsy and Jagger appeared in the supper room, one with a look of wicked triumph and the other grinning like a horse.

I was still not all that pleased with either, but Maggsy announced, "Found 'em, or leastways got word of 'em, you tell him, Jaggs," and Jagger took up the tale. "Got down here from the Salisbury coach last Sunday, riding outside, and the ostler recollects 'em as he reckoned the lady was a kind of foreigner, though speaking English plain enough."

"And the gent then asks for a chaise and post-boy to carry 'em on to Romsey," Maggsy continued. "And it seems that's close by where we're bound for."

He paused, for he always liked to keep the tidbit for the end, and I said, "That's what we might expect by now. Did you find the post-boy?"

He nodded. "Which we done. And the post-boy recollects 'em also, as he heard the lady observe that she don't like this part of the job, and they don't know which church it is neither; nor it seems they don't just know where they want to go, so the post-boy put 'em down at The George. On which the gent pays out the hire, gives him a sixpenny bit extra and then asks how many churches there is in Romsey. To which the post-boy replies that he ain't precisely sure as the sight of a whole sixpence all to himself addles his wits."

"And very like a post-boy," I observed. "They're all rascals. "Was there any more?"

"Never satisfied, are you?" Maggsy inquired. "But not much save this cove's got a brace of pistols as well. The post-boy put 'em in the chaise with the rest of the baggage, and not a lot of that. So what d'you make of it?"

"You'll see for yourself if you think for a bit," I told him. "And it looks as if you'll have to find out for yourself how many churches there are in Romsey as well. And very likely visit all of 'em."

"We might have knowed it," he announced. "That's all the thanks we get, Jaggs. But what we want to know is are they after our Peggoty or not? And come to that, where is she? You ain't let her go rollicking off on her own, have you? You know what these places are."

"She's been sent to bed with a good respectable chambermaid to keep her out of mischief." I was becoming somewhat vexed by Maggy's constant fussing over the child. "And she's not *our* Peggoty now. She's Miss Amelia Lydia Clarissa Pangersbourne, and don't you forget it. For the rest, it certainly looks as if they're after something which concerns her, but don't forget neither that she's not to be told anything of this or what we're about. She's a chatterbox and she's bound to know some of these folk at Milton Pangersbourne. I don't want her blabbing our business to all and everybody before we see which of 'em, if any, we can trust. And now," I concluded, "We'll have a nightcap and then take ourselves to our own beds. I'm looking to another early start tomorrow, Jagger my lad, with our horses and the chaise bright and shining for it."

So to make short work of the rest of it we set off again at six on another fine sunny morning, had the highway to ourselves and paused only for refreshment at The George in Romsey while Jagger went about his mysterious confabulations with the ostlers there. And here one thing became clear that I had suspected last night from the post-boy's observations: *viz* that our gentleman and lady were running short of money, or at least of immediate funds. "Engaged the cheapest chamber there was," announced Jagger as we took the road once more, "bread and cheese for their suppers, and went off afoot the Monday, and never a shilling to anybody."

And with a sailor's sweet farewell from all, I reflected, if I know anything about the manners of innkeepers and ostlers. "Was there any more inquiries about churches?" I asked, but Jagger shook his head on that, saying not as he'd heard, and seeing that Miss Amelia was showing signs of a lively interest I said, "Let it be, then: let's be on our way, and keep the horses brisk but steady."

Passing on from Romsey and approaching Lyndhurst we now found ourselves passing through the glades and thickets of the New Forest, and some of 'em damnation wild and desolate; pretty enough in the sunlight, but a fit place still for highwaymen and other wandering villains at night. Here a desolate heath and there a dark grove of ancient trees or a precipitous hanger, now a herd of deer flying away from us and again a bunch of wild ponies; in one place two or three black-faced charcoal-burners watching us with evident dislike as we passed, in another a gang of tinkers, and as wicked a looking gang as I've ever seen, in one more a gipsy encampment, with its mangy-looking lurcher dogs, vans, tents and horses, and bold-eyed wenches. Jagger touched up his horses to get past 'em the quicker, keeping his whip handy, and Master Maggsy muttered, "I don't fancy the look of that lot." No more did I.

For some time Miss Amelia had been growing more and more pensive as we drew closer to our destination, and she was particular thoughtful as we left the gipsies behind and came to a leaning signpost which announced, 'Deadman's Mill ½, Milton Pangersbourne 1 Mile'. Then without a blink of warning she asked sweetly, "Uncle Sturrock, why are we coming here?

You'll have to tell me in the end, so you might just as well tell me now."

Maggsy sniggered evilly and I was so put out that for a minute I was at a loss how to answer the deceitful little wretch, and the low female cunning to have been quietly considering the question all this time and only now to ask it.

"We've come for the visit," I said firmly. "And perhaps to see if we can find out something to your good. But you are not on any account to tell anybody I'm a Bow Street man, as that often makes people uncomfortable. If you're asked you may say I'm a reporter from *The Gentleman's Magazine* come to write a piece about the cricketing men of Hampshire." It was a most suitable subterfuge, as I had lately been reading an article in that journal about the late Mr Richard Nyren and the Hambledon Club; while, as I have noted elsewhere, I follow the fortunes of the Marylebone team and can keep up the chatter with the fancy. "So see you mark that," I told her.

"Yes," she said innocently; but looking uncommonly thoughtful. "If it's cricket you've come about," she added, "You must talk with Mr Ironband, the blacksmith, as he's a famous cricketer; when he doesn't have his Trouble on him. And of course the Reverend Hangbolt. Although when I see Mr Hangbolt again I shall beg leave to spit in his eye," she observed in the most genteel of accents.

"Come, my dear," I reproved her, "You're getting on for being a lady now. You must forget your Wapping manners. But tell me," I asked, "wasn't there some disagreement between your grandfather and the reverend gentleman?"

"My oath, there was," she said with another touch of the Wappings. "And right fierce. It was several years

33

since and Granpy was one of the umpires in a meeting between the Pangersbourne men and Wittings End. The Reverend Hangbolt was pitching the ball, and Granpy declared one of the Wittings men not out when the Reverend cried 'Howzat sir?', and the Reverend said he was, and Wittings End won the match. And the Reverend said Granpy had done it with intention because a gentleman at Wittings End had received some strange new plants from the Indies, and Granpy was hoping he might be given two or three of them."

"Sounds more like Wit's End to me," Maggsy muttered, while I asked softly of the Lord what sort of place had we come to, but further discussion was then cut short by Miss Amelia announcing, "And this is Deadman's Mill."

And a well-named place it looked, for I never saw one so ill-favoured. Mr Constable would never have fancied that one. A heavy construction in black timbers and overhanging eaves like beetled brows, openings under them as might have been empty eye sockets, and a great weed-beribboned undershot wheel turning, creaking, groaning and slapping at the rushing flood in the leat. The mill pool a sullen sheet even in the sunlight, not a ripple on it, but patches of evil green here and there, and stretching away to a thicket of dark trees on the further bank. "Anybody wants to drowned himself, he couldn't choose better," Master Maggsy observed; "I reckon that lot's got as many ghosks as black beetles," and indeed as we rattled past I caught a glimpse of a whitened face peering after us from one of the windows.

Even Miss Clamaity glanced back at it somewhat fearfully, and I said, "Let's hope to God the rest of the place is a bit more cheerful. If the inn's anything like that we shall have a damnation odd lodging."

As it happened the inn was neither all that bad, nor all that good either, being a low sort of thatched place, but bigger than might have been expected, fronting on the green—where there was a gaggle of geese and sundry ducks keeping the grass down—and opposite half a dozen or so various cottages, with the church tower poking up among the elm trees at the far end. It had a decently red-riled floor to the tap or common room, and the pewter was well sanded, but on the other hand the landlord was a squint-eyed rascal who professed never to have heard of claret, or not to have any. Nor was he any more accommodating at first in the matter of lodging, for the arrival of so many travellers and especially the sight of Miss Amelia Lydia seemed to throw him into a deep suspicion. "You'd do better at Lyndh'st," said he; "back the way you've come."

I was about to tell the fellow's fortune for him in no uncertain terms, but fortunately his wife proved a woman of a more sensible nature, though rough-tongued. She was about three times the size of him, with tits like a pair of pumpkins, and she announced, "You'm a fool, William Oakes. Money's money, en't it? Even if it do come with a Pangersbourne by-blow," she added, gazing at the poor sweet child just as unfavour-ably, and asking, "So you've come back, hev you? We'd heard as you'd been took off by the gipsies and sold to a circus; if nothing worse."

"Parson wun't like it," the amiable Mr Oakes started, but she cried, 'Then Pa'son can bliddy lump it. I shall have to do the work and empty the pots, not him nor you."

"A poor welcome, mistress, but better than none," I observed, resolving to get the better of this precious pair before I'd done with 'em, and so the matter was arranged. Me in a chamber above the tap, where I damned near cracked my skull every time I straightened up, Miss Amelia in a little garret under the thatch, and Magsy and Jagger in the stable loft. Needless to say Master Maggsy complained most bitterly; but Jagger was content enough, for when he can't get a chambermaid he'd just as soon sleep with his horses.

Rude as it was, however, I soon perceived that this chamber had its own advantages. Its floorboards were laid simply on the rafters of the taproom below and, being of old timber, there was considerable cracks in between 'em, so without putting yourself to much trouble or indignity you could hear pretty well every word that was said down there, and I lost no time about the job once the woman had left me to myself. While we were coming to our agreement in the tap I had noted two ancient yokels sitting in their smocks by the window, though had not paid much attention to them, but now it seemed they were in animated discussion with Mr Oakes—or what passed for animated among these bucolics—for one was asking, "Where d'ye racken her be from, Willyum? And what's her after then?"

By the sound of it Mr Oakes was busy banging the pots about, but he replied, "Buggered if I know, Aaron. But he've got the look and stink of a lawyer about'n. And buggered if he'm going to stop here no longer nor I can help it neither."

There was silence for a minute while they pondered that, until the other observed, "Lawyers'll be proper bad mischief here."

"That's sure to be right, Moses," the one called Aaron agreed at length. "And worse'n mischief with that liddle maid come back with'n. Nonetheless, Mrs Oakes be a powerful woman to cross."

"And that's sure to be right likewise, Aaron," Moses

36

announced after further profound reflection. "But so's Parson Hangbolt powerful to cross as well. An' a wicked ole devil with it when her starts. I rackon 'tes black mischief either way."

"Be damned to yer endless chatter," said Mr Oakes, banging his pots again. "Never quiet for a minute, you two. Demanding a pint of claret as bold as a bliddy lord," he added, and then asked, "Where's Ironband? I ain't heard the smithy ringing yet today."

"Gone to Ringwood, so 'tes said," answered Aaron after another minute, somewhat put out.

"To see about the match come Saturday," Moses finished for him. "To find out ef he can ef Slogger Barnes be striking for them rascals."

"Aye, there's the match," Oakes muttered. "Can't have nothing come athwart that." He continued, "But ef they get at Ironband . . .' and then stopped short, for on that moment Jagger must needs come roaring into the tap crying, "What cheer, gaffers all; I'll have a pint of ale, Landlord," and what further revelations might have been made will never be known.

Hard on that also sundry bumps, thuds and curses on the stairs heralded the arrival of Master Maggsy dragging up my valise and announcing in his dulcet manner, "God's weskit, I don't like this lot all that much."

"Keep your horrid voice down," I admonished him. "I fancy every word we say can be overheard. Where's Amelia Lydia?"

"Gone round the green to look for the blacksmith." The wretch peered down at the floorboards and gave his wicked grin. "I see what you mean. It's handy, though, ain't it?"

"It might be." I listened for a minute to Jagger below saying that I was a famous sportsman and writer on

37

cricket, and then continued, "Then fetch the child back. I don't want her ever left on her own if we can help it."

"Like that, is it?" He bent down to look out of the window. "She's just coming back. She's right enough for a minute, watching the geese. And I got a tasty bit for you first. There's a stable-lad here. Ain't much more than sixpence in the shilling, but he can answer simple questions, and I reckoned I might as well ask him about that gardener we're after. Thomas Grubbage. Seems he was what this lot call a foreigner here, no relations, and a cantankerous old villain."

"What d'you mean," I demanded. "Seems he was?"

"Ain't no more," Maggsy said simply, still watching through the window. "Stable-lad didn't want to talk all that much, and Thomas Grubbage can't, as he's in the graveyard; though the stable-lad says there's some reckons he don't always stop there. He was found in the mill pool a twelve month back, just after the old lord took his fit. So what d'you make of that? Did he dive or was he pushed?"

But before I could offer any observation on that there was a fearful honking of geese from outside and he screeched, "God's Whiskers, them things'll eat her if she ain't careful," and went galloping across the boards and down the stairs like a herd of wild elephants. While at the same time Mrs Oakes's little more melodious tones came echoing up, "Mind what you're about, you little demon; and if you up there want your dinner you'd best come down to have it." So once again further revelations and discussion was postponed.

I am bound to say that the dinner exceeded all expectations. After that damnation duck and gallstones at Blackwater I feared even worse here, and in the noble words of our immortal Dr Samuel Johnson, 'I look upon it that a man who does not mind his belly will hardly mind anything else'; but whatever the weight of that monstrous woman she had a touch as light as an angel with pie crust. A venison pie with rich gravy—the meat no doubt poached from the Forest—a choicely ripe Dorset Blue Vinny cheese, which you cannot get for love nor money in London, and a nearby wine made of plums that very near took the top off your head. It was fine, simple country fare and I lost no time in complimenting the excellent good woman in the most generous terms; which, though they did nothing to lessen her voice, clearly pleased her.

So refreshed and strengthened we next set out to investigate the village, the graveyard and any other matters of interest, keeping Maggsy and Miss Amelia with me and sending Jagger to look for the smithy in case there should be an apprentice or something of the sort idling there. The two ancient gaffers was by this time sitting side by side on a bench outside the inn, seemingly dozing though watching everything, the cunning old rascals, but otherwise there was little sign of life save for the aforesaid geese. In short the village was sunk in slumb'rous peace, but now under a strange and brassy light, for the sky was growing sullen and the air sultry. Even Maggsy and the child of calamity were unwontedly silent as she led us past the cottages and up a little side lane to the churchyard.

Here there was a handsome lych-gate, the mouldering memorials to the rude forefathers of the village and a somewhat more impressive urned and pillared mausoleum which I took to be the last resting-place of the Pangersbournes, all embowered in sombre yew trees, etc. The church was of a style and size above what you might expect in a place like this, as Dr Wilford

Caldwell had observed, and the vicarage—a little way off to one side, and also embowered in trees and mantled with ivy—likewise seemed of a sort that must have been a most comfortable living at one time. In short it was such a scene as might have inspired the late Mr Thomas Gray to one of his meditations; even to another ancient figure, leaning on a scythe, who might have been the Last Reaper himself.

But seemingly he wasn't after us, or not yet, for he knuckled his forelock politely; and putting these reflections aside I sent Maggsy off with Miss Amelia to look for Thomas Grubbage, if he could be found, while I went to the Pangersbourne tomb. This was more a matter of curiosity than anything, as I did not expect to glean much information, but there were certain surprises when I came to study it. Not least a considerable list of names engraved in he stone, some of 'em half obliterated, so there must have been a fair number of the family stowed away in there.

It was the last three, however, which provided most food for thought; the first of these being, 'Lydia Clarissa, beloved wife of Edward, Fifth Baron Pangersbourne, 1763–9 November 1783'. The next was 'Roderick Edward Everard Pangersbourne, Lying in a Foreign Field, 7 November 1782–1809'. And the last, cut roughly in the stone, as if by a mason who did not trouble himself to finish the job decently, said simply 'Edward Everard Henry, Fifth Baron Pangersbourne, 12 December 1759–8 July 1814'.

"So ho," I mused, pondering on these inscriptions, 'we've tragedies enough here, God knows. The wife dies at twenty, the son at not yet twenty-seven. And surely Pangersbourne was a youngish man to fall to an apoplexy at only fifty-five?"

But at that moment Master Maggsy called to me

softly from a little distance off, where he was standing by a more modest headstone. Miss Amelia I noted had withdrawn as far as the lych-gate, and was now gazing back apprehensively at Old Father Time with his scythe, and when I trod my way through the grass to Maggsy he muttered, "She don't fancy it a lot here; you can't hardly blame her. She's fearful the Reverend Hangbottle might come roaring out, though I've told her that with me beside her she's got no need to fear nobody. And that old hunks with the slasher's been watching every move we made. But take a look at this. That's your cove all right. And somebody's done him proud."

And indeed somebody had, seemingly the same mason, for he had granted this stone several more words than he had vouchsafed Lord Pangersbourne. 'Here lieth Thomas Grubbage', it announced, 'who set many plants to earth in his time, and is now set to earth himself to await the Harvest of the Lord. 11 July 1814'.

"Another observation as might have come from the pen of Mr Gray," I said. "And only three days after Pangersbourne."

"What're you considering now?" Maggsy demanded suspiciously. "I hope you ain't reckoning on digging that one up. I don't fancy some of your habits, and he's best left where he is."

I shook my head. "I doubt he'd tell us much if we did. If it came to a choice of the two we might do better to have Lord Pangersbourne out; though there wouldn't be a lot to be gleaned from him by now, either. I'm merely wondering why somebody here should put a headstone to a man reputedly cantankerous; a foreigner, so called, and of no kith or kin to his name."

"There's no telling what this lot might do," Maggsy announced, looking back at the Ancient Reaper. "So

41

let's get out of it. That old curiosity's hobbling off towards the vicarage."

Being a man of the nicest delicacy, and not wishing to arouse painful memories in the child—though, to tell the truth, also thinking that the answers would not be worth the trouble—I had never so far pressed Amelia Lydia with too many questions; but now there were some which had to be asked. So when we came out, to her undisguised relief, I said, "Well, Amelia, we don't need to linger here. Shall we go and look at Pangers-bourne House next? If you'll show us the way."

She was not all that pleased with this invitation either, for she answered, "It's up this lane a bit further. You come to some big iron gates. You'll find them easy enough. I'll go back and talk to the geese."

"You'll talk to us, and let's have no nonsense," I announced, for I cannot put up with being crossed by a child.

"If I must," she said unwillingly. "But if you mean to make me come back here to live, I won't. I like it much better with Maggsy and Mr Jagger and riding in the chaise. And you, of course," she added generously.

"And we like having you," I assured her. "So tell us something about your grandfather. Was he just as kind to you?"

"Well, yes," Though she seemed somewhat doubtful. "When he remembered I was there. I was mostly with Mrs Coggins: the housekeeper. Or Mother Gossive. Mrs Coggins always told me I was a child of misfortune, and she didn't know what was to become of me."

Maggsy muttered something wicked under his breath and I wondered who the devil Mother Gossive was. But there would be other ways to find that out and I asked,

"What kind of build was your grandfather? Was he of a heavy and corpulent nature; fattish? Liable to sudden rages, and of a flushed face; protuberant eyes?"

This time she looked puzzled and Maggsy kindly explained. "Bulging out. Like organ stops."

She shook her head again. "He wore spectacles, so they couldn't could they? He was quite thin, and tall, and stooped a bit. From studying too many books, Mrs Coggins said. And nothing like flushed, ever; nowhere near as flushed as I've seen you sometimes, Uncle Sturrock."

So even more unlikely to take a stroke, I mused. "And what was your grandfather's manner with the gardener: Thomas Grubbage?"

"Thomas Grubbage?" she repeated in purest Wapping undefiled. "He was a right old bleeder. He said he'd got a vegetable in the plant house that'd eat me all up if I went anywhere near it."

Maggsy snickered, but I reproved the wicked child sharply. "We'll have less of that if you please. Pray remember that you're no longer in Wapping. What was your grandfather's manner with Grubbage?"

She turned a trifle sulky again. "Mother Gossive likewise said he was a rare right old . . . Mrs Coggins said he took too much on himself. But Granpy thought the world of him."

Maggsy looked at me sideways, but by this time we had come to a pair of tall wrought-iron gates, once handsome, but now half open and starting to rust. Beyond was a drive and a stretch of parkland, with some nice stands of timber and bushes set out after the manner of Mr Capability Brown, and at the end a pretty, elegant mansion in the style of Queen Anne; not all that big against some I have seen—and even visited, most notably my good friends Lady Dorothea

43

Hookham-Dashwood and Sir Tobias Westleigh—but still a commodious country seat of the landed gentry. But all showing evident neglect. The grass in the park pretty well knee high, the trees and bushes unkempt and weeds encroaching on the drive, moss starting on the stone and brickwork, the windows blank and vacant, and much of the glass broken.

In short, a melancholy spectacle, with the afternoon lengthening and the sky growing heavier, and I was moved to a touch of the philosophies as we approached along the drive. " '*Naturem expelles furca, tamen usque recurrent*', as the poet Horace says," I mused, for I like a good bit of Latin when I can hit upon the proper observation. "Or in the vulgar tongue, 'Though you drive Nature out with a pitchfork, she will always come home to roost'."

"So long as she ain't the only thing roosting here," said Maggsy. "As I see something move across one of them windows just then."

"What?" I demanded, while Miss Amelia let out a squawk. "Which window? And what was it?"

"Dunno." We were at the foot of the terrace steps then, and Maggsy was still peering up at the house like a pointer with his snout twitching. "Nothing there now. Just a sort of something, and didn't seem to be looking at us. First window to the right above the door."

"Most likely a caretaker," I said.

"Not so," declared Amelia shrilly. "Mrs Oakes at the inn says there's nobody. She says nobody from the village will ever come near. And that room was Granpy's special private study where he had all his books and did his writing."

"Then it's somebody who's got no business here," I announced, "and we'll soon see what he's after."

"Not me," she cried. "I ain't going in there. And

don't you go neither, Uncle Sturrock. Mrs Oakes says . . ."

"Be damned to Mrs Oakes," I cut her short, "and Mrs Coggins and all your other female fearfuls. Stay here with her, Maggsy," I said, starting up the steps.

Even as I spoke a wicked splat of lightning ripped across the sky, followed by a fearful rattle of thunder as I took the half dozen paces across to the portico. Miss Amelia loosed off another screech just as I noted that the door was ajar an inch or two, and when I turned an instant to look back she was plucking up her skirts and taking to her heels along the drive as fast as her fat little legs would carry her. Maggsy was standing there like a gumkin, not knowing which way to turn, and I said, "Be damned, get after the silly chit," pushed the door open wider and passed boldly inside.

THREE

It was a smallish hall, darkish and strangely cold after the glowering light outside. A black and white tiled floor, a table and three or four Hepplewhite chairs, a few pictures on the panelling and faded squares where others had been taken down, and at the far end the two wings of a staircase going up to an open landing or gallery; all pretty elegant though not palatial, and all dimmed with a film of dust. And in the dust there, two sets of footprints; one pair square-toed and small-heeled like town boots or shoes, and the other broader and not so well shaped, such as the footwear of these country clodhoppers. "So ho," said I, "so much for ghosts," then pausing to listen, for there was the strangest little sound coming from somewhere above. Tap, tap, tap, and a pause; tap, tap, tap, and another; and then once more, tap, tap, tap. "And that's no woodpecker either," I observed softly, making my way across to the stairs.

The window to the right, Maggsy had said, and it was easy enough to find, for once on the landing the corridor ran straight right and left and there, pretty well at my hand, an open door with the tap, tap, tap again, a muttered curse—uncommonly pretty—and a most

46

interesting spectacle within. It was, or had been, a study or small office, and now not only in neglect but also in the wildest disorder; papers scattered everywhere, books taken from the shelves and tossed on the table and chairs, the drawers of the desk turned upside down on the floor; and a fellow dressed in town clothes, with at least the appearance of a gentleman, rapping at the panelling with his knuckles.

So engrossed was he that he did not notice me and I stood for a full minute watching him, observing from the dust and disorder of his dress that he must have been sleeping damnation rough of late, and having no doubt who he was from Mr Sims's excellent description of him. Then I asked, "Captain the Honourable Wilberforce Haggard, I presume?"

He came about all standing, gazing at me with his jaw damned near dropping off before he got out, "Who the devil are you? And what're you doing there?"

Not a very practised villain, I reflected, though certainly reckless and therefore more dangerous. "Why," I said, "pretty much the same as you, I fancy. And a rare confounded mess you've made."

"The place was like this already," he started, and then confirmed my opinion that he was a fool by thrusting a hand within his coat and coming out with a pocket pistol. "What're you after?" he demanded.

"Come now," I told him, "don't let's have any pranks with that thing. It might go off. Moreover I don't talk business with a pistol pointed at my guts."

There is nothing catches a rascal's attention quicker than that simple word, and he asked, "What business?"

"I might know where to find what you're looking for." In fact nothing was further from the truth, for I did not even know what it was. "But I don't give information for nothing. So you tell me something first.

Did you find the entry of Roderick Pangersbourne's marriage in the parish records of Romsey? Some time about 1802, and to a woman signing herself either Clarissa de Champillion or just plain Clara Comfrey."

If possible his jaw fell even lower. "God's sake, how in damnation d'you know we was in Romsey at all?"

I gave him what Maggsy calls my hanging-judge smile, the which had frightened the bowels out of many a harder villain than this before now. "You'd be surprised at what I know. Did you find such entry? If so in what church? And how did she sign herself?"

The poor fool was so dumbfounded that he even let his pistol hand drop, and I half thought of stepping across and taking the weapon off him, but concluded against it for fear of upsetting him. "How in damnation . . ." he repeated.

The fellow was a gentleman, I reflected, or had been at one time, for I had seen many like him brought down by horses, cards, women or all three; and although the room was growing dusky as the sky darkened I could make out that he was handsome in his way; sun-tanned as if by much travel, yet a weakish kind of face. A man I wouldn't trust in a tight corner, and I did not trust him now, for he jerked that damned pistol again and demanded, "What's Clara Comfrey got to do with you?"

"That's a nice question," I answered. As indeed it was, for if there was a record of the marriage it would prove whether Amelia Lydia was a bastard or not; though it might also mean that the woman would claim her if she thought there was property with the child. "So did you find the record?" I asked. "Is she Clara Comfrey or Clara Pangersbourne, and where is she? Is she the woman you're travelling with?"

"Be damned, you want to know too much," he said.

48

But then I perceived his eyes go past me, and at the same instant another spiteful flash of lightning distracted my attention. Too late I heard a movement behind and caught a stink of sweat, horse and wood smoke. The fellow cried, "Hold hard, Tickner," but even as I turned to defend myself my beaver was swept off, a crashing blow fell on my unprotected head and I descended in a coruscation of firmaments; though not without a most heartfelt curse.

Was there ever such a situation? A man of my experience to be taken by surprise like a virgin in a whoreshop, for I had failed to consider that other pair of footprints in the dust though I had seen 'em plain enough; and I hardly dared to contemplate the sniggers and guffaws should Master Maggsy and Jagger ever get to hear of the encounter. But I could not have been out all that long, for I had a notion of rude fingers rifling through my pockets, heard just as rude footsteps making off in haste, and then a voice bawling from below, "Hulloa there!"

I answered with certain observations that might have startled a hackney driver and heaved myself to my feet, adding several more as I discovered that my pockets were turned inside out and my gold watch and purse gone, and then stemming my eloquence for a minute as another figure appeared in the doorway. A widebrimmed clerical hat, under it a face as red as a round of beef and much resembling one otherwise, and a long black burial cloak; a pretty sight in my present state of mind. "And what's about, sir?" this apparition demanded, "and what are you doing here?"

I was growing uncommon tired of these same questions by now and I informed him so in no uncertain terms until he said, "Pray moderate your observations, sir," and I paused a minute for breath. "What does it look like?" I asked. "Two damned villains. One searching this place, and then they set upon me. And absconded with my watch and purse. Did you see 'em?"

His eyes went past me to the disorder in the room and it struck me that he was not all that surprised. He said, "Aye," half to himself, and then, "I saw two fellows making off along the terrace as I came up the steps. Tinkers or gipsies. They're a pest about here. But that don't say what you . . ." He broke off as there was a further rip of lightning and added, "Come, sir, there's a storm beating up. It's holding off yet, but it'll be heavy when it starts, and if we don't wish to be caught . . ."

"Quite so," I agreed, "but a minute first." In fact it was only the work of a moment to examine some of the open pages of the books and papers lying about and see the light film of dust here too. So that fellow had been telling the truth: this room had been comprehensively searched already, at least some weeks or even months since. But the reverend gentleman—clearly Parson Athanasius Hangbolt—was watching me frowningly, and I observed, "The literary bent, I fear, sir. I cannot see a collection of books anywhere but what I must needs peer at 'em."

The expression on his face plainly called me a liar. Despite his beef appearance the Reverend was nobody's fool, but he made no further comment until we were descending the stairs; and then he inquired, "Does your literary bent also extend to studying tombstones?"

"Why not?" I retorted. "I have often considered composing a meditation in the manner of Thomas Gray. It appears to me that your churchyard would make an admirable subject for such an exercise."

There was no doubt that he perceived the double meaning in that, as I intended he should, but again he said no more until we came to the outer door. Then, however, he next asked, "This door, Mr Sturrock. Was it open when you entered?"

"It was," I told him brieffly. "And, as you will observe, there is no key in the lock. Is that a curious circumstance, I wonder?"

"It may be," he answered after a pause as we passed down the steps and out to the drive, not in any undignified haste, but keeping our eyes on the darkening sky.

But by now it was my turn. "You seem to be singularly well informed. "My name and my presence in your churchyard. And here in the house."

"News travels fast in a place like this," he observed. "And here's another curiosity. I'm pretty certain that I've seen your name elsewhere of late. I fancy in *The Times* newspaper."

And that was the devil and damnation. For that estimable sheet had carried a most complimentary report of my recent doings with the smugglers and pirates of Wapping—before mentioned in the matter of *Captain Bolton's Corpse*—in which I had been plainly referred to as the ornament of Bow Street; or words near enough to that effect. If these suspicious rascals of villagers got any wind of that we could kiss our hands goodbye to any hope of discovering what devilment was afoot here; even if we did not find ourselves run out of the place with certain other portions of our anatomies kissed to help us on our way. And this bullock of a parson would help 'em do it.

Nevertheless I carried it off neat enough. "It's not unlikely. I sometimes commit an opinion or two to paper, and now and then the editor does me the honour of publishing them. But I fancy you're more likely to have seen the name in *The Gentleman's Magazine*. If your news travels complete as well as fast you'll be aware that I'm engaged to write a piece on the cricketing men of Hampshire for that journal. And I propose to make particular reference to your match with Ringwood this coming Saturday. I heard that spoken of in The Bat and Ball Inn, at Hambledon, a few days back."

"Indeed?" His tone was somewhat dry. "I would not have thought our fame had travelled so far."

"Further than you think, sir," I said. And it might go further yet, I added to myself.

There was a thoughtful silence as we turned down the lane towards the churchyard, but anybody might have guessed the next question he was itching to ask. There was another flash of lightning and a closer roll of thunder; he murmured, "The rain still keeps off, but we shall have it any minute now." I replied, "I fear we shall." And then he got it out. "The late Lord Pangersbourne was a friend of yours?"

"Well, no," I admitted, for the truth is always best when it can't be avoided. "I never met the gentleman."

"No?" He paused again, plainly uneasy. "Then the child, Amelia? You'll pardon my curiosity, but we all here had a deep affection for her; as we still have. In a sense I was in *loco parentis* to her after the tragedy. And when she was lost, with a band of gipsies so far as we could discover, we were all profoundly concerned. The most exhaustive inquiries were made; though to no avail."

"I've no doubt they were," I agreed warmly. "And it does you credit. So you want to know how she comes here in my company? And very natural. You'll be acquainted with the Hookhams, of course? The old Duke of G—. Prodigiously wealthy, sir, all of 'em. Lady Dorothea Hookham-Dashwood is one of my oldest and dearest friends, and I'm a regular visitor to her *salon* in Hanover Square, London. A bit on the Whiggish side, between you and me, but uncommonly influential. And, of course, Mr Dashwood's a Member of Parliament; you'll certainly have noted his name in *The Times*. Well then, Lady Dorothea's presently travelling in Italy, and the climate there's considered unsuitable for a young girl."

"I see," the Reverend said shortly, though it was very clear that he didn't, and was not likely to; but there was enough in that to make him or anybody else here tread careful if they happened to be contemplating any oddities. Now by the lych-gate he paused again, looking up at the lowering sky and starting, "You'll take shelter in the vicarage . . .?" but on that instant Maggsy and Jagger appeared round the corner from the village and the rain started coming down in splats as big as florin pieces. It was a fortuitous moment for polite farewells, and I said, "Thank you, no, sir; I'll make a dash for it. You'll not wish to be encumbered with my clerk and coachman."

When I went to the vicarage I meant to be the party who asked the questions.

Back in my room however, and not all that wet, I put the one I was already getting sick of. "Where is she?"

"In the kitchen," Maggsy answered. "With Mrs Oakes. Helping get the supper ready."

"Begod," I said, "that's unwise. There's worse mischief here than we thought, and by the look of it it's damned ugly mischief. If she starts chattering we don't have a chance of getting to the bottom of it."

He shook his head. "She won't. We've got an understanding, me and Peggoty. I told her that if she blabbed a word of who we are and what we're here for—not that we know that ourselves, do we?—we'd see that she

53

stops here for good and never comes nowhere near Soho Square no more. That sobered her. Being a woman she might fancy she can wheedle you, but she knows better than try it on me. She won't split; she's more like to find something out." He was studying me somewhat curiously. "And what happened to you? You're looking a bit greenish."

"A mere slight accident," I told him shortly, at the same time thanking God that it was no worse, and that like any prudent traveller these days we had a good reserve of coinage in a secret part of my valise. "We've more important things to think of," I added, and asked, "What's down below now?" for there was a steady growl of conversation coming up through the floorboards.

"Dozen or more in there," Jagger said. "Kind of meeting."

"Then we can talk without being overheard," I observed. "But keep your voices low. So what's your report?"

"Not a lot. Blacksmith Ironband's got an apprentice, but he don't say much. One remark about every other minute. Forge wasn't alight, and he was sitting on the anvil communing with himself, and I says where's Mr Ironband as I might want a job done. To which he replied 'Gone to Ringwood to find out who the Ringwood men are putting in the field on Saturday'."

The good fellow gave me his horse's grin: a fearful sight but well meant. "So I next henquire which side should I put my money on, and he says that depends on which of the Ringwood men Pangersbourne can nobble, but they don't know till Ironband gets back and he ain't come yet. Which is rummy, as he borrowed Parson's hoss to ride on and was to be back by middle afternoon to report to the Parson. So I observe that it looks as if the Ringwood lot might've nobbled Ironband instead; which the apprentice then says it's unlikely, as Ironband's an uncommon powerful man, and the only one as can ever nobble him is Mrs Ironband, who ain't no more than half size to a pint but a rare holy terror, and it's more likely that he's got his Troubles on again."

He paused for breath and Maggsy observed, "That's the second time today we've heard of Ironband's Troubles. Though by the look of it they've all got troubles here." He turned his attention to me. "And by the look of you there was troubles up at that house as well."

"I've told you," I said, 'a mere slight accident," and the look in my eye warned him off a touch of the sniggers. I went on to the rest of my tale and when I had finished he asked, "So if this cove was Captain Haggard what was he after? Them title deeds to America?"

I shook my head. "I can't think they'd mean much after all this time and the Independence. But it's something to consider. And it's certain that rascal was searching for some secret hiding-place."

"And the tinkers or the gipsies in it as well." Maggsy pondered that for a minute. "So who's the woman who was with him at Whitchurch and Romsey? God's whiskers, it couldn't be that Clara Comfrey, could it? Our Peggoty's mother; or supposed to be?"

"I asked the same question myself," I confessed. "But recollected that in Romsey they asked how many churches there are there. That means they didn't know which one they wanted. But it looks as if they were seeking a record of the marriage."

He took the point quick enough. "Meaning further that if it had been Clara Comfrey she *would* have knowed; as it's an uncommon forgetful woman who can't remember which church she was married in."

"There you have it. So it's more likely that they are or have been acquainted with Comfrey, though not all that close. But if there is a record we must find it ourselves. I'll have you and Jagger ride back to Romsey one of these days to take a copy of it and get it witnessed. We might have need of it."

"I dunno about that," Maggsy announced. "I dunno that we shouldn't do better to leave this alone. It sounds as if this Clara Comfrey's mixed up with a damnation oddsy lot, and more than like to be damnation oddsy herself. If you ask me we shan't be doing Peggoty no favour to find her."

But on that Jagger said, "Hold your hosses." He was now peering out of the window, and he added, "Parson's heading over here."

"So what now?" I asked, bending to look out of the window myself. By this time the thunder had grumbled off into the distance, but the rain was still coming down in ramrods and the reverend gentleman was a mighty figure breasting through it, marching by a path acrosss the green under a vast black umbrella with the skirts of his cloak flapping about him like a bat. "That cove means business," Maggsy muttered. "And God A'mighty important as well if he comes sploshing out in this lot."

There was a sudden silence below as he entered the tap, and then Oakes started, "Good evening, Parson," sounding somewhat uneasy, while the Reverend replied, "A very wet evening, but I'm pleased to see so many here, for I've several things to say to all of you. Thank you, Oakes; I'll take a mouthful of claret."

"That'll be half a gallon by the size of him," Maggsy whispered, and I breathed, "The lying villain Oakes, he said he hadn't got any." But Oakes was next saying, "I had to do it, Parson; I tried to turn 'em away, but you know what Mrs Oakes is," and the parson answered, "Indeed I do; indeed we all do; a very worthy woman."

That fetched a bit of a snigger, though still uneasy, and he continued, "We'll come to that in a minute. First, however . . .' He paused, and then announced, "The keys to the House. As you all know, they hang in the vestry for safe keeping; where they can be shown if any duly authorised person should ever ask for 'em. Or they should hang there. But they're not there now, and it seems plain that one of you damned rascals has purloined them."

There was a further uneasy silence at that. Maggsy was lying flat on his face with his eye to the widest crack in the floorboards, and he whispered, "God's weskit, I don't wonder Peggoty says she'd like to spit in his eye." Then the parson continued, "I don't ask why or who has them, and I don't want to know, but I mean to have 'em back. That's for everybody's sake. So whichever has them will bring 'em after dark. And if he's afraid to enter the churchyard—as you all may well be considering your manifold wickedness—he may leave them on the seat of the lych-gate. Am I understood?"

Seemingly he was, although a confused murmur came up. Maggsy shifted his position, muttered, "Some of 'em's saying something about Thomas Grubbage and the old lord," and the reverend rascal once more went on, "Now to the other matter. The strangers we have here."

On this the mutter became an ugly growl, with several of them voicing their opinions on what to do with us, and none of very kindly intent. It became a perfect babel until Landlord Oakes snarled, "Stow it, yer bliddy fules," and the parson cried, "Silence! You're a pack of idiots. What good d'ye think you'll do with dung heaps, or the mill pool? We've had trouble

57

enough out of that already." This brought a sudden dead quiet, and he added, "Let me hear no more of fowling-pieces either. You'll bring a hornet's nest about your ears."

But the rascals was still argumentative. One of them again muttered something about Grubbage, and another replied, "All the same us wants to know what they be after, parson, harnet's nest or not." By the horrid creaking of the voice it sounded like old Aaron. "Be that'n a lawyer, think you? Her've got that wicked inquisitive look about her, and me and Moses watched her in the churchyard poking and peering where her shouldn't have had no business to peer. 'Tes a harnet's nest anyways if her be a lawyer, and fearful trouble for all."

"Fearful trouble indeed, Aaron Copley," the parson agreed. "And more than time enough for all of you to contemplate your sins. I'll tell you plainly, I don't know yet, though it's certain the man's about more business here than cricket. But I mean to find out. I've come across the name Sturrock somewhere else of late, and it won't take me all that long. But for now my advice to all of you is to be courteous and circumspect with him, and with the other two, but otherwise keep your mouths shout. In simpler words, give them good day and good evening, but don't answer any questions and don't ask any."

The buzz rose again, but there was no doubt the parson was their master. Nevertheless one other of them asked, "What about the liddle gel, pa'son? The liddle Pangersbourne bastard? What's she about here along of 'em?"

"We don't know that either; not yet." For the first time his unholy reverence himself sounded uneasy. "The child's harmless. There's nothing she can tell

58

them."

"Ain't there, though?" This one seemed a bolder villain than the rest. "But liddle pigs have got big ears, and 'twas her who first told Mother Gossive about that fearsome vegetable." This brought a fresh murmur, and the wretch continued, "Axing your pardon, Pa'son, and all respec', it seems there's an a'mighty lot you don't know, and us can't afford to be fanciful. She were took by the gipsies once, and I say it'd be no bad thing if she was took again. They'd do it for a guinea or so, which Samuel Oakes here could cover easy enough; and it'd pay him to."

"You speak for yourself," Oakes started, but the parson came in again with a voice of hell-fire. "Silence!" he said again. "And let me hear one more word like that from you, Jonas Smallbrook, or from any of you, and I'll see you all to the Assizes myself. Apart from wicked it'd be a mistake and dangerous. We'll have no more talk of that sort. And bear in mind about the keys. I want 'em back, and I strictly forbid any of you to enter that house again."

"Be damned if us wants to," another growled. "Leastways I don't. Niver know what might ketch you."

"Then that's just as well," the parson rejoined. "Whatever tales you've heard there's nothing there worth the harm that might come of it. Now let us turn to other matters. Is there any word of Ironband yet?"

That seemed to end our present interest in the discussion—though I was growing anxious to have a word or two with Blacksmith Ironband myself—and a fine kettle of mysterious herrings it sounded like. "A pretty parcel of rascals," I observed softly, while Maggsy whispered "Mark that Jonas Smallbrook, Jaggs. The runt with a scar down his chaps, and looks more than

59

half a gipsy. If he means any mischief to our Peggoty we'll have his tripes out for it."

But on that the child came dancing in, announcing at the top of her voice, "Supper's ready, and I helped to make it; ain't that clever of me?" There was another sudden silence below, and Maggsy hissed at her, "God's sake, keep your screech down." He added, "If they rumble we was listening to 'em . . ." and I finished for him, "It'll be an interesting situation. You'll get us into trouble before you've done," I told the little calamity. "But let's go down and see what's waiting for us."

It was a stuffed and baked pike, caught from Deadman's Mill pool, Mrs Oakes informed us; a dish much recommended by Mr Izaak Walton, in *The Compleat Angler*, as being a meat too good for any but anglers or other very honest men, but I thought it curious rather and somewhat bony. Master Maggsy muttered that considering the mill pool and Thomas Grubbage he didn't altogether fancy his, but with that and several other oddments we made a fair enough meal nevertheless; and needless to say I was once again lavish in my praises to Mrs Oakes.

Once again she was plainly gratified, although she told me to go along with myself, and when we had finished and at my command Amelia Lydia, Maggsy and Jagger was set to work to clear the table, I kept her aside for a private word. "She's a sweet and biddable child," I started. "Now and again. But we all know a girl of that age can easy be a vexation about an inn. Yet she can't be with me or my clerk and coachman all the time."

She cut me short. "Are you asking if she'll be looked after?"

"I am," I answered , straight and simple.

"She will," she said, just as brief.

She busied herself about some small task for a minute, stood listening for another to the hum of conversation from the tap across the passage and at last continued, "So long as the child's under my roof she'll be safe enough; whatever she may be. She'll stop with me until it's time for her bed, and then she'll be sent. But I'll give ye one last word. There's other childer about the place, and you know what childer are. They get queerish notions of their own, and they can easy be put up to things."

"I take your point," I told her. "And I'm obliged to you. But there's one more question if I might ask it."

The excellent woman gave me another hard look. "I can't stop you. Though that en't to say I shall answer it."

"It's very simple. Who is Mother Gossive? And where may Mrs Coggins be found? Lord Pangersbourne's housekeeper."

"Mary Coggins and Mother Gossive?" She turned suspicious again on the instant. "What d'ye want with them? You won't find neither. Mary Coggins was a Dorchester woman, and she's gone back there. As to Polly Godsave, God only knows where she is now. She was buried on the parish last winter time."

Damnation, I thought; there goes another one. But I said, "Now that's vexatious. How did it happen?"

"Took of her chest; being near enough seventy, and lived in a hovel in Deadman's Copse, back end of the mill pool. She was a witch, or so some said; but kind to the child in her way. And rare powerful with herbs and suchlike. Gathered 'em from the woods and fields, and a sight better physician than that bliddy fule Birdlip at Wittings End. What did you want of her?" she asked again.

61

"Why, merely to thank her for her kindness," I said, somewhat more thoughtful still. And on that note I finished the conversation and called Master Maggsy and Jagger from the kitchen to come with me to show ourselves in the taproom.

Dr Johnson has observed that there is nothing which has yet been contrived by man, by which so much happiness is produced as by a good tavern or inn; but he had never met such a company of rascals as was gathered in this one. About a dozen and a half of 'em, I reckoned, of all shapes and sizes and a different order of rascals from the sort met in The Brown Bear in Drury Lane—where they are mostly honest thieves, dips, riggers, receivers and suchlike—but a sort of lowering bucolicity and sullen looks; and a fearful stink of wet frieze, rank tobacco, pigs, cows and dung. In short, particular tasty, and a profound silence fell again as we entered. "God's whiskers," Maggsy muttered aside, "if this is what they're like when the parson tells 'em to be courteous I'd hate to see 'em when they're feeling rude."

Only Aaron and Moses piped up, "Evening to ee, masters," with one adding, "I could rare fancy another pint, Mr Oakes, ef you'll be so kind, but I don't jest hev the pennies about me."

"Then we've come just in time," I announced, though counting the cost, "ask the company what they'll take with us, landlord." Upon which you never saw such a hasty emptying of pots and holding them out; but at least when the clamour had died down Mr Oakes offered, "I can find ye a drop of claret now if ye fancy it."

"Indeed I do," I told him warmly. "Your country ale's a bit strong for my head." Then when that was served, I added, "Well now, here's to your match on Saturday. But what will your wicket be like after this downpour?"

"Wet," one of 'em said.

"Spinner Wildgoose be a bugger on a wet wicket," announced another.

"Ar," several more agreed in chorus. "Her be."

"Worse nor a bugger," Aaron observed. "I mind the day as her broke the skull of a Wittings End man."

" 'Tes true," said Moses. "I mind it as well."

"Come now," I rallied them, "it'll make a more interesting game. What're you playing for?"

"Why, to see which side wins," answered Moses after further thought.

" 'Tes true," said Aaron. "I rackon that's what we'm about."

"I mean what's your wager?" I explained kindly. "There was a time when the Hambledon men played a match for a thousand guineas. And another for a stake of eleven pairs of white silk britches and eleven pink silk shirts. Now that was cricket."

"So's our'n," one more spoke up. "Our'n gets bliddy murder sometimes." He pondered on that for another minute, and then added, "Most times."

"You want to go easy," Maggsy muttered in my ear. "You'll get 'em animated before you've done. And mark that little runt with the scar down his chaps."

I nodded while draining my claret—and sour-gut stuff it was too—glancing at the fellow over the top of my pot; a foxy face little rascal with the bandy legs of a life-long horseman, watching us with weasel eyes. "I have him," I murmured softly, for that was Smallbrook; the rogue who had proposed putting Amelia Lydia off with the gipsies again, and he spoke up then himself for the first time. "Be any of ee cricketers,

63

master?" he inquired with a wicked leer.

Jagger was now putting on his horse grin and the sight of it inspired me to a pretty piece of sporting mischief. I said, "I'm a mere onlooker. But my coach-man here's a very different matter. He's uncommonly well thought of by the Marylebone Club." I doubted whether they had ever heard of that august body, but I added carelessly, "He's too modest to tell you so himself, but there's few can tame a fast bowler more surely. If it happenes that you need another man, and you ask him the right way, I daresay he'll carry a bat for you."

I never saw a grin vanish quicker in my life. Jagger started, "Here, for God's sake," for there was no mis-taking the sudden interest in the good fellow. Given another minute the rascals might have fallen into a perfect babel of conversation, but Maggsy was half killing himself with a struggle not to laugh and I judged it was time to leave. "Well then, we'll give you all good-night," I finished. "We'll take a turn round the green to study the wicket."

Once outside, however, Jagger gave full vent to his feelings. "God blast it," he demanded, "what of damnation did you want to say that for? I ain't never held a cricket bat in my life, and well you know it. Nor never wanted to. They'll have my guts out for it. You heard what them villains said in there. Cracking skulls, and their notion of cricket's bloody murder. And if you don't stop hooting and pissing yourself," he added to Maggsy, "I'll crack your skull to start with."

"Come, my lad," I reproved him, when he stopped to take a breath. "I thought you were a sportsman. It's what we call establishing good relations. They'll not play you in their team. They ain't as mad as all that. Or if they do they'll only put you in as the last man. It'll all

64

be over in a minute or two."

"My oath it will," Jagger cried fervently, while Maggsy let out another hoot.

"Have done with it, the pair of you," I said dragging them apart. "I've more to tell you yet."

I then continued about Mother Gossive, or Polly Godsave, while we walked under the elm trees in the thickening twilight. The rain had stopped now and there was a sweet aroma of damp earth in the air, with other poetics, etc., but the sky remained heavy and there was still grumbles of thunder and a flash now and again. Lights in the cottages, women at the doorways taking the air, some of their children clustering about them; and all watching us. A pretty rural scene, save that from the direction of the smithy there rose a shrill voice announcing to the Heavens what somebody there would do to Master Ironband when he did choose to come home. "And they're all up to mischief," I observed as I finished my tale.

"You reckon somebody done this Polly Godsave as well?" Maggsy asked.

"I don't reckon anything presently. But it all hangs about this horrid vegetable Pangersbourne was cultivating, though I fancy there's still more to it. Recollect also that this old woman was a herbalist of sorts, and there's a lot of herbs that're not all that good for the bowels. To be plain about it, we've never had a mystery of quite this sort before and we've a mess of investigations to make. But in particular we must discover if there was any inquest or inquiry made on the deaths of Pangersbourne, Thomas Grubbage and the woman Godsave."

"Meaning me and Jaggs," Maggsy said.

"Meaning you and Jagger can drive over to Wittings End tomorrow. You'll find out all you can about a certain Dr Birdlip. And you may take Amelia Lydia with you for the outing. It'll keep her out of harm's way, as I shall be busy in Pangersbourne House. And for that I shall want the keys."

Maggsy stopped short. "Meaning I get 'em for you. Oh no," he declared. "Not bloody likely. There's been three knocked off here already, and I don't aim to be the next. Besides it'll be bucketing with rain again any minute, and if some of this lot don't gut me I shall catch my death of cold."

"Then if it rains it'll be a good dark night," I retorted. "I want those keys to use as and when I think fit. If we're to get to the bottom of this business I must examine the papers in that study."

FOUR

It was as black as the ovens of Hell. The comfortable townsman who never ventures into the wilds of the country can scarcely imagine how dark it can be, for in London the better shops and houses put out lanterns on brackets, and there are always carriage lamps and torches passing by. But here you could not see the nose leading your face when I went out after Maggsy and Jagger; and true to Master Maggsy's forecast it was starting to spit with rain once more.

The plan was very simple. Maggsy and Jagger had returned to their stable loft and clumped about as only they can, while I had done much the same in my own chamber above the tap. Then after a short interval they had crept down again as silently as cats; Maggsy to secrete himself in the yews by the lych-gate, Jagger a little distance off in case of need and me as a sort of rearguard. I was by no means certain of what we might achieve apart from getting the keys, but I had a notion that we might hear something or perhaps witness some curious doings.

But for the present there was not a light anywhere, the entire village seemingly wrapped in slumber, and not a sound save the drip of rain from the trees and the cry of a melancholious owl as I made my way to my own position; a rough, open-fronted cart-shed on the other side of the green and close by the end of the church lane. By the nature of its position the open side was facing the cottages, and in proposing to go round and shelter inside I must needs approach it from behind; and fortunate that I did, or I might have spoiled everything. For as I came near I caught a whiff of the rank tobacco these country rascals affect. There was already somebody within, so nothing for it but to edge up to the boards at the back and conceal myself as best I could, in a damned uncomfortable situation with the droppings from the low thatch running down my neck.

The rain started to come down heavier and I made several observations under my breath. The church clock struck eleven, and seemingly the other fellow was just as impatient as I, as he made several more similar comments; but then I caught the light crunch of footsteps on the road, and he whistled softly. One strange canting voice said, "Here we be then, lovey-dearie, the wagon-shed by Timbrell's old cottage," while the other—which I recognised as Captain Haggard's—required, "Is that you, Smallbrook? What the devil d'you fetch us out for on a night like this? God's teeth, it's as black as the Pit."

"So much the better," Smallbrook replied. "That suits you best, don't it? And keep your voices down. There's other folks abroad; or there's something abroad. I heard a muttering from the churchyard."

Master Maggsy confound him, I thought, but the canting rascal gave a whinnying snigger. "Very likely, Thomas Grubbage. They say he walks on wet nights."

"You stow that, Abel Tickner," Smallbrook hissed. "That's mischancy talk," and I whispered to myself, "So ho, so it's Thomas Grubbage they're fearful of," but Captain Haggard said, "Be damned to this. What did you feetch us here for? Your boy merely said something important."

"So it is," Smallbrook growled. "But I couldn't say too much, as the parson's on his high horse. It's Oakes and the keys. Hangbolt says to give 'em back, and that's what Oakes means to do. He daresn't offend Hangbolt; there's none daresn't offend him for fear of what he knows about 'em."

"The keys?" Captain Haggard demanded. "What the devil's Oakes about? Didn't you tell him only to open the door and then leave the keys there for me?"

"To be sure I did," Smallbrook answered. "But her rackoned her'd do best to keep 'em to herself till you paid'n what you promised."

"It's a damned confusion," Haggard started, but the gipsy now whined, "What's keys to us, lovey-dearie? There's never a house built that can keep Abel Tickner out. We can get in there whenever we've a mind."

"You can't get into what I'm looking for. I've told you, it wasn't in the study, where it should be." He was growing ill-tempered and seemed to turn on Smallbrook again. "Has Ironband come back yet? And who's this other fellow sniffing about? A damned puffed-up bull-frog."

"God knows, but her's up to mischief; that's certain," Smallbrook said. "And there's something else, master." He gave an evil snigger, but then stopped sharp and added, "Quiet now; her's coming."

I just caught it myself, a glimmer of light on the far side of the green, come and gone as if a door had opened and closed, and Smallbrook whispered, "That's Oakes. Her'll go up along topside, and if ye want them keys now's your chance to have 'em."

"Then for God's sake let's go," said Haggard, and

69

thereupon all three moved off to the accompaniment of a flicker of lightning, while I observed, "Be damned, another minute or so and I might have learned more. And if they happen on Master Maggsy and Jagger lurking up the lane there'll be some fireworks. Moreover," I added, "That damned gipsy villain might still have my watch about him. And a damned puffed-up bull-frog, am I?"

So it was a situation which seemed to demand my particular attention, and keeping on the grass I followed softly after them. By now it was raining rods again, a fit night for villainy, and they was well out of sight in the blackness, nor did I try to catch up with 'em yet, though they was still muttering between themselves. It was something about me and the child, I fancy, for Haggard seemed to be asking questions, but by this time they had turned the corner of the lane and I paused here to find my own reinforcement. "Jagger," I murmured into the dark, "are you there?"

There was not so much as a whisper of an answer, and I started, "Be damned, if the villain's failed me I'll have his guts for it," but hard on that there was several commotions ahead. Still not a thing to be seen, but first somebody sneezed; and it sounded like Maggsy. Then a fearful voice demanded, "God's sake who's there?" and another answered in low and hollow tones. Next a strangled screech of utmost terror, a kind of jingle and a horse laugh which was my excellent Jagger for certain. And right on all of it a rattling crash of thunder, another fearsome screech and a spiteful flash of lightning that lit up Maggsy peering from the lych-gate like an imp out of hell, Jagger pissing himself with laughing, our three fine rascals hunched together like conspirators and Landlord Oakes galloping down the lane with his arms flung over his head like a demented drayman; and all in the ramrods of rain. I never saw anything more horrid at Sadler's Wells. It was enough to turn your stomach over.

Then blessed darkness returned, and the gipsy villain bawled, "Treachery!" Not to be outdone Haggard roared, "Damn your eyes, Smallbrook!" and banged off a pistol; Maggsy uttered a further screech of his own and Jagger emitted a bellow of rage. Where the Honourable's ball went I know not, but by the uproar they was making they all sounded healthy enough, and when a further flash revealed a somewhat confused altercation now going on I felt constrained to join in myself; and with no niceties. As many a lady will know, you can't be too particular when fighting in the dark, but I shall not sully these genteel pages with any of the observations that was being bandied back and forth.

One of 'em must have struck Smallbrook down, for he was rolling, cursing and kicking on the ground, clutching rudely at whatever came handiest, Oakes was fighting such devils as he knew not what and not a little discomposed, and Jagger and Maggsy were engaged in a curiously confused mêlée with the other two. I fancy I trod on Smallbrook's face a trifle carelessly, as he gave out a doleful shriek and ceased his transports suddenly, while Oakes exclaimed again that something was getting at him, broke away in a perfect frenzy and cantered off into the gloom.

Then, however, that murdering gipsy rascal turned round on me with the glint of the knife in his hand and I quite lost my patience. The wicked weapon ripped my sleeve, but at the same time Providence chose to send a further flash of lightning to my aid, just enough to show him to me, and I came up with my right to his chin, and round hard and low with my left to his nether parts. It was an unsporting blow but gratifying, for the fellow went down with a wheeze like a punctured organ bellows, whereupon I first banged his head on the gravel two or three times to keep him quiet, then tore his filthy jacket apart to go through his pockets; and sure enough the rascal still had my watch tucked in his moleskin weskit. "And we'll have that back to start with," I observed.

And just at that juncture a fresh voice demanded, "What of God's name is this?" and I looked up to perceive the flapping bat's-wing skirts of that damned burial cloak, the wide hat and the parson himself, holding a lantern in one hand and a horse pistol in the other. Smallbrook gave a dismal moan and scuttled off on all fours out of the light; my own fellow started to kick again, took me by surprise and got away after him; Jagger and Maggsy stopped short in the act of quietening the Honourable, and he took his chance to fling Maggsy aside, deal a wicked blow at Jagger and then make his own escape. "Be damned," I cried "Stop that rascal, I want him!" but Jagger was flat on his back and cursing; Maggsy replied, "Stop him yourself," and the Parson announced, "Brawling at the very gate of my churchyard."

"What is this?" he demanded again. "And what are you doing here, sir? Are these your town manners?"

"It'd take too long to tell you, sir," I retorted. "But, in short, taking a walk for a breath of air before retiring; and set on for no reason by a gang of your damned rascals. And if these are your country customs, I don't like 'em."

"Taking a walk?" he repeated, "In this weather? Come, sir, you must think . . ."

"I'll tell you what I think in due course, sir," I promised. "And I'll tell you at some length. But for the present my thoughts ain't fit for clerical ears, and I'll beg leave to give you good night."

So we left him with his lantern and marched off down the lane; wet, muddy and not in the best of tempers, Maggsy and Jagger still making various observations, me thinking that if we could have kept Captain the Honourable much might have been explained though at least I had recovered my watch; or *a* watch, for it seemed somewhat different and lighter than my own. That was a matter which could wait however, and when we got to the corner we paused for a minute in case of further attack. But all was dark and still; seemingly if any of them here had heard that pistol they were keeping in their beds with the covers over their heads; all was quiet save for the piss of the rain, and I said, "Well enough then. Where are the keys. And what happened?"

"I snooze," Maggsy growled. "Blade of grass tickling my snitcher, or I've already catched my death. And I suppose you know that was Landlord Oakes? He says, 'God's sake, who's that?' and I answer, 'Thomas Grubbage, and it's bloody wet down here'. It was the only thing I could think of; and not surprising neither."

"I know all that, or can guess it," I told the wretch impatiently. "Where are the keys?"

"I dunno," he replied. "He dropped 'em, and all Hell come loose."

"What?" I exclaimed. "You blue-arsed, pig-snouted ape. After all our trouble and danger. We lose two villains who might've answered questions, and you leave the keys there as well."

I paused for breath, fearful of a stroke myself, and of all people Jagger saved. me. "Hold your hosses before you take a fit," said he smugly. "Not fancying to fart about on my own I went along close behind Maggs. And that cove didn't drop 'em neither, he proper flung 'em away, and I catched 'em. I reckon I might be better at this cricket than I ever thought of. Anyhow, I got 'em right enough."

"Then you've saved the situation, my lad," I announced. "And we've defeated that damned parson, who I'm beginning to conceive a dislike for. We can go to our beds, and we'll all have a nightcap on the way to drive the wet out."

But that proved to be easier said than done, for when we got across the green to the inn it was closed, shuttered up, bolted and barred, and as dark as all the rest of this pestilential village. No amount of knocking, rattling, entreaties or imprecations produced any effect until at last a window opened above our heads and the great moon face of Mrs Oakes appeared above us. "Take your bliddy selves off," she said.

"Come, madam," I protested, "we're chilled and wet."

"You'll be a bliddy sight wetter in a minute if you stop there," she declared: upon which the unspeakable creature leaned out with an escessively common domestic utensil in her hands, Maggsy screeched, " 'Ware pots!" and we dodged back just in time to avoid a most unsavoury deluge. The cry and such rude antics are still by no means uncommon the Seven Dials, in London, but I had hardly expected to encounter them in the kindly countryside, and I told the woman so in no uncertain terms; though to no effect for she had already withdrawn and slammed the window. And I thought I heard Miss Peggoty give a giggle, the wicked little wretch.

I made several other observations, but it was Jagger again who saved us. Seeming to be unseasonably amused, he said, "I'll see to it," and led the way round to the stables, where he rattled on the doors and cried cheerfully, "Open up, Pig's Arse. That's what I call the stable-boy; he seems to reckon it's a compliment," he explained, as a sleepy voice within called back, "Who is it?" and then continued, "I daresn't; she'll kill me if I do."

"And I'll kill you if you don't," Jagger promised, just as cheerful. "Come on, now. It's a shillun for you one way, or I'll have your liver out the other. You can't keep a man away from his hosses."

On that plea, common to horsemen the world over, the doors were opened a crack just wide enough for us to get in, disclosing a horrible little boy as much straw and muck as humanity, though he held his hand out fast enough for the shilling. One way and another the expenses of this expedition was mounting up to a pretty proportion, but I paid philosophically, and the creature returned to his bed in the hay, while Jagger further led the way up a devilishly rickety flight of steps and struck light to a candle to reveal a poky little loft. Nevertheless it was better than a night under the elms, I reflected, and when the good fellow even produced a bottle of the plum wine—little less warming than brandy—I very near promised I would raise his wages; but thought better of it just in time.

So divested of our wet and muddy outer garments and our comforts more or less improved we turned to consider the events of the evening as we passed the bottle round. "And Thomas Grubbage first," Maggsy said. "I reckon I done a most important discovery there. For if Master Oakes gets as screeching paralysed as that at the thought of his ghosk, it looks as if *he* cooked him."

"It's a thing to be considered," I agreed. "Though I fancy it's not quite so simple if we're to believe the report that he was drowned in the mill pool. Which we've no reason to doubt so far. Recollect that the parson declared they're *all* afraid to go into the churchyard at night, and have reason to be. So did they all have a hand in the affair?" I shook my head. "I don't see it. Or are they all merely ignorant, superstitious bumpkins, and was he frightening 'em for reasons of his own? It's a certainty that that horrid cannibalistic plant or vegetable comes into the matter somewhere; but for the rest we don't know yet. And we're baulked because we can't ask questions here. We wouldn't get any answers if we did, though I mean to try Ironband when he does appear. So for now let's take a look at those keys, Jagger."

The good fellow passed them over, but at first sight there was nothing very particular about these either. Eight of them in all on a big ring, and all clean and well kept. Four of them pretty modern, not unlike my own domestic keys for Soho Square, two more heavier and somewhat older; and the last two very heavy, curiously wrought and very old. "So ho," I mused. "Here I fancy we might have something. For unless I'm much mistaken these are the keys to an ancient strong-box or chest."

In themselves, however, the keys could tell us little, though they put certain ideas into my head—for these inspirations come to me naturally—and the greatest surprise was the watch. Maggsy glanced at me out of the corners of his eyes when I took it out, and I said testily, "Yes, well, in short I lost my watch by mishap this afternoon, and I had hoped to recover it from that gipsy villain. But . . ." I added, and for once in his life he had the sense to keep his mouth shut, "But this ain't mine."

To tell the truth it was even better. A very fine timepiece in gold, though a trifle fancy for my taste, elegantly chased on the face and back, a bit worn from usage though plainly well looked after. "So ho," I mused again, opening it up, "how did the villain get this, and who and where from, I wonder?" and some part of the answer was there to see. Engraved on the inside of the outer case were the initials 'H. G. de Bourne", while on the inner cover protecting the movement, very small and barely visible in our candle light, were the words 'Frémont, Richmond, Virginia'. "So ho," said I for the third time.

"All right then," Maggsy grunted. "All this so-hoing. So he dipped that from somebody as well. Very likely an habit he's got into. Or does a touch of the highwayman now and again."

"I wonder?" I asked, but Jagger the sensible fellow yawned cavernously and inquired, "Won't it wait till the morning?" and I said, "Indeed it will. Let's get what rest we can for what's left of the night. We've a busy day before us tomorrow; and I suspect it might be troublesome as well."

And troublesome it was, after a damned uncomfortable night with one thing or another, and Maggsy and Jagger snoring an angel's serenade in chorus. I was thankful when the clacking of hens and a clanking of pails signalled a happy new morning in this peaceful village and lost no time about putting on my outer garments, damp as they still were, and descending to the fresh air. At least the rain had passed off, though the sky was still lowering, and so was Mrs Oakes' side-of-bacon brow when I found the inn door now open and discovered her mopping out the taproom floor. For a minute indeed I fancied that she was contemplating wrapping the mop around my chaps, but I gave her a polite good-mornig, to which she instantly inquired, "What's good about it?"

77

"That remains to be seen," I observed. "But where's Mr Oakes now? I wanted a word or two with him."

"Took to her bed," she announced briefly. "And by the look of her won't never be the same man again. Not that anybody'll not grieve all that much if her aint't. But there's mischief here, master; and you've brought it. I'll thank you to pay what you owe, and be off."

"Mischief there certainly is," I agreed warmly, "and damned ugly mischief when an innocent traveller and his clerk and coachman are set upon by a dozen and more damned ruffians while taking a quiet stroll. My two men are nervous, peaceable fellows. They're not used to such things, and they're afraid for their lives."

"They're what?" she demanded. "I never saw a wickeder-looking pair of rascals in my life."

"And they won't thank you for that either," I told her. "But let's have no hard words. I'm a forgiving man, and it looks as if you've got your own troubles, whatever they may be. We'll have a wash and shave, some dry clothing and breakfast, and then be off to Wittings End."

"Wittings End?" she repeated. "What d'ye want to go there for?"

"Why, to find another inn," I replied. "I don't mean to have my tour of the Forest cut short. Though I doubt we shall get cooking anywhere near as fine as yours, and I fancy the folk there'll be almighty inquisitive as to what's so much amiss here that you turn good money away; as I am myself. But it's no business of theirs or mine." That took her well between wind and water, and trusting in the frailty of ladies to forget today what they told you yesterday I continued, "I've a visit to pay there anyway. A Dr Birdlip, who's a friend of another friend of mine. I've never met the gentleman yet, but I'm told he's a notorious gossip, and much interested in some strange plant or vegetable or the other."

The good woman fell into the trap like a kitchen into cream. "Dear Goda'mighty," she whispered, started, "You don't want to believe a word . . ." and stopped short. "Nor what that lot at Wit's End . . . They'm all rogues there, and them that ain't rogues're simple." She stopped again, and then added, "True enough, 'tes good money. And there's a batch of nice crusty bread fresh-baked yesterday. And I daresay I can find a rasher or two of gammon, and a bowl of eggs. But there's no tea."

"Be damned to tea," said I. "A quart of ale apiece'll do us better. And here's a guinea on account to see if you can find us a plump young duck or two for when we get back to our dinner."

So having come to an understanding we made a pretty fair breakfast—with Miss Amelia Lydia still inclined to giggle when she looked at me—and then set off about our several businesses; myself to ride in the chaise with Maggsy and the child until they were past Deadman's Mill, when I proposed to get down and make a circuit back through the woods in the hope of reaching Pangersbourne House unobserved. It was still early when Jagger brought the chaise out, but there were one or two women at the doors of their cottages, a knot of men seeming somewhat anxious and another woman holding forth outside the smithy—from which it appeared that Blacksmith Ironband had still not yet returned—and several of the dreadful children gazing at us with their eyes goggling.

And then arose a small incident which put me on the track of the mystery, or at least one part of it; for, looking like a perfect small lady in her sprigged muslin and bonnet, Miss Amelia chose to put her tongue out at the infants, whereupon one of them promptly picked up a stone and flung it at her. It might well have chipped our paintwork or struck one of the horses, with God knows what results, but before Jagger could reach for his whip or even I could remonstrate the sweet child screeched, "You lay off that, Johnny Peascod, you little bastard; I told you what I'd do for you before."

Needless to say Maggsy was hooting with wicked laughter, but one of the women screeched back and the situation began to seem quandarious. "Be damned," I said, heaving the calamity into the chaise, "let 'em go Jagger, before we have a riot on our hands," and we clattered off in a hurry with sundry cat-calls behind us. We were passing the mill before I finished an improving lecture on genteel behaviour, the manners expected of a lady and so on, with Maggsy still cackling, and when I stopped for want of anything further to add he asked mischievously, "Anyhow, and after all that, what did you offer to do for Johnny Peascod?"

"I told him I'd set Granpy's horrid vegetable on him, and it'd eat him all up," she answereed defiantly. "But that was a long time ago."

"However long ago it was you should have had more sense," I reproved her. "These country people brood on things like that." But by this time we had arrived at a place which looked suitable to my purpose, out of sight of the mill with woodland at both sides of the road, and I said, "You may put me down now, Jagger; and meet me here again at two o'clock. In the meantime go careful and no racing; remember all my inquiries, and don't get into mischief; and for God's sake don't let her get into any either."

So they went off again in festive mood, Jagger carolling one of his sporting ditties, Miss Amelia Lydia waving her ribbons at me as they swept round the bend, and I set out to find my way through the forest.

I shall not report a lot on that expedition, as somewhat
to my surprise nothing happened and so far as I knew
then I was unobserved. I had a fair notion of the lie of
the land and by my reckoning it was little more than a
mile or so, far enough for a townsman maybe, but ample
time for certain philosophical reflections on the singu-
larities of Nature, etc., and in particular the hordes of
damnation, pestilential, buzzing, biting flies in the
humid air; which put me in mind of that mysterious
plant of Pangersbourne's, the Venus's Fly Trap. In
short I had my thinking-cap on, turning over several
items that I'd seen and heard, while my eyes were busy
noting comfortable farms with cattle grazing here and
there where the paths led through open spaces. But so
far as I could I kept to the cover of the trees myself and
with these useful occupations it did not seem long
before I came round to the ha-ha ditch and wall which
marked the boundary to the Pangersbourne park.

This was at the back of the house, and beyond the
boundary there was another stretch which had already
grown wild and neglected before I came to a further
wall, a gate set in an arch but now falling off its hinges,
and a considerable enclosed garden. It had the look of a
botanical interest about it, with separate narrow beds
divided by paths—such as I had once observed at the
famous Chelsea Physic Garden when visiting there with
Lady Dorothea and a party of her scientific friends—
though now in disorder and overgrown by weeds. This
was a matter more for Dr Caldwell than me, I concluded, but I noted also a row of melon pits and their
covers tossed aside and broken, two plant houses with
the glass likewise smashed and doors hanging loose, and
other signs of wilful damage.

81

Beyond this lay the stable yard, once pretty commodious, having accommodation for half a dozen cattle and several carriages, but now as empty as a whore's heart; not so much as a scrap of harness or even a wheelbarrow to be seen. Next came the rear premises and kitchen quarters, these somewhat surprisingly in better order, with all the lower windows shuttered and the doors sound and solid; and here I set to work with the keys, trying one after the other until the main door swung open with a cavernous creak. And not unlike a cavern inside, for as I stood there listening for a minute there was a dank silence about the place which struck me chill.

Nevertheless I had work to do and wasting little time on the sculleries or kitchens—though from a few brief glimpses at the disorder here it looked as if the inhabitants had left in a hurry—I passed through to the main apartments and hall. Sooner or later the entire place would have to be searched from top to bottom, with or without authority, but I was already getting a notion of what had happened here just over a twelvemonth past, and my main concern for now lay with that study on the first floor. There, if anywhere, among those papers, I should find my best information about Lord Pangersbourne, the condition of his finance and perhaps the state of his health at the time of his death.

But it was a damnation mess up there, the door still open and all lying as I had left it yesterday with the parson after my unfortunate mishap. It would be a long job and no point in tapping the panelling like Captain the Honourable, as you can play that game for a month of Sundays and never find anything unless you know what you are looking for. Neither were the books worth much more trouble, a hundred or more of 'em, all of a scientific or general horticultural nature—such works as the *Systema Naturae* and *Genera Plantarum* of Carolus Linnaeus, and Miller's *Dictionary of Gardening* —for it was clear that they had already been very thoroughly searched, seemingly for some document that might have been concealed within their leaves. What I was after, or at least a hint of it, would be contained somewhere in the papers scattered about, and I set to work gathering up and sorting them.

Letters by the dozen, a number from gentlemen of the Horticultural Society and several more from correspondents of similar interest in America. One dated January 1814 from no lesser person than Thomas Jefferson himself describing the garden he was continuing to lay out at Monticello, and finishing, 'I am gratified to hear that you continue in robust health, as do I in spite of increasing age and the present wintry weather here'. Another from a James Hunter, in March of the same year, thanking his lordship for his generous contribution towards the costs of an exploration 'beyond the Missouri River, as the expenses of these expeditions increase as it becomes necessary to travel further afield'. And then one more of November of the year before from the Hampshire County Bank 'Respectfully advising His Lordship that consequent on his draft of 100£ to James Hunter Esqre, Philadelphia, his remaining credit was now in the sum of 105£ 5s 9p'.

In short, and in the light of what Dr Caldwell had told me, there were sums here which did not seem to add up, especially when I discovered and arranged in their order a number of commonplace or day books going back as far as 1795. They appeared to be records of Pangersbourne's experiments with plants and seeds received from his various correspondents over the years, but unfortunately there were no less than five of them, all very near as big as ledgers, and the minutes were flying.

I had no time for more than a quick turn-over of the leaves, though still time enough to observe two other matters of interest; first, that he had subscribed regularly to expeditions to the Americas and the West Indies, and second, that latterly these subscriptions had increased in size rather than lessened.

Plainly there was fresh food for thought in that, but I put the books aside to continue my examination of the other papers and now a further curiosity came to light; for there was no sign of any correspondence from lawyers or agents and no rent rolls or estate accounts that you might expect to find in a gentleman's study. What remained seemed to be trivia, but here too I discovered two other items; one being a number of scrip or share certificates in the old South Sea Company, and the other a map of the estate. At first I very near tossed both aside as being too old and out of date to mean much, but something—I can only conclude it was the touch of Providence again—prompted me to consider them more carefully.

What else it could have been I know not, for the share certificates had been issued in 1719 and '20 and the map—hand-drawn, with some parts marked off in red, and signed 'William Hawkins, Agent'—was dated 1714. But when the Finger of Providence prods me in the ribs I never ignore it; and, as I could not stop to study these documents now if I was to meet Maggsy and Jagger at the appointed time, I stowed them away in my pockets to take away with me and prepared to leave.

FIVE

Whatever Providence might have done for me within the house, however, He chose to leave me to my own devices when I got outside again. I have frequently reflected that He gets these absent-minded fits now and then. The place was still sunk in that dank silence as I descended the back stairs—pausing for a minute at the kitchens once more to survey the disorder there—and there was not so much as a cat or rat stirring in the stable yard. Nor was there any movement in the enclosed garden, only the same silence, and the sky darkening for further rain before long as I made my way down the paths between the strange flowers, plants and rank weeds. But as I got to the outer gate to the stretch of parkland beyond a twig cracked in the bushes nearby; and but for that and my own quick movement I'd have got my head blown off as neat as a whistle.

It must have been an old-fashioned fowling-piece. There was the snap of a flint, the spit of priming; and I just dodged back behind the wall a bare half instant before the crash of the explosion and a blast of shot which fetched a cloud of dust from the brickwork. "Be damned," said I, somewhat non-plussed, torn between my instinct to go out after the villain and common

85

prudence to stay where I was. And prudence won for, brave as I am, I am not a fool and nobody but a fool shows himself when the other man is under cover and waiting for him; but I wished I had my own Wogdons with me. I'd have shot the rascal to hell.

As it was I remained pressed against the inside of the wall, trying to get a sideways glimpse over my shoulder and through the archway in case he should show himself, while a voice from somewhere deeper in the park cried, " 'Ware shooting there!" On that the bushes rustled, seemingly this fellow here retreating, as at the same time another voice called from the stable-yard end of the garden; and I turned now to perceive none other than Dr Wilford Caldwell approaching. "Why, sir," he cried, "what was that? Did I hear a shot?"

Just for once I was very near impolite to the good gentleman. "You'd be deaf if you hadn't, sir, for it went off like a cannon. Merely some damned rascal had a try to blow my head off. Waiting for me, with an old flint-lock fowling-piece by the sound of it."

I fancied I caught a gleam of uncalled-for amusement in his eyes. "Well now," said he, "that's alarming, is it not? It seems you must have upset some of 'em already about there."

"It appears more than likely," I agreed. "And not surprising, for the place is a perfect nest of villains. And I'll upset 'em a damned sight more before I've done," I added, but then stopped short, looking back at the archway to the park in further astonishment.

Between surprise and the impudence it very near took my breath away, for who should now appear but Captain Wilberforce Haggard and a young woman with him. For a minute we all stood at a loss for words, until I found my tongue first, as I usually do, and demanded,

86

"What the devil do you want here? What's your business, and who are you? And was that another of your villainous friends?"

"That shot?" He paused to glance at the fresh scars in the brickwork, raised his eyebrows and then had the further impudence to grin at me. "Begod," said he, "the fellow must have loaded it with nails. But no friend of mine. We saw somebody scampering off, roughly dressed and trailing a musket. A common poacher, after a pheasant I thought, but shooting wild in these bushes. That's why I called out to him."

"A likely tale," I retorted. "That rascal was waiting, and there's no doubt you posted him there. We had a tussle with you last night, my man, and you were quick enough with your pistol yesterday."

"And could be again," he said. "And if it comes to asking my business here, I might just as well ask what's yours?"

The insolent jackanapes stared me down as bold as brass and had not the woman intervened I hesitate to think what might have happened next. My neckcloth was damned near strangling me, I started, "By God . . ." and the fellow looked like answering back, but she shook her head warningly at him and said, "We ask your pardon if we trespass, sir. As you may perceive we're strangers here, and seeing this old garden and the empty house we thought no harm to come in to look at it."

Dr Caldwell, I noted, was studying her with some interest; and not surprising, for she was of a shapely figure and melodious voice. A pleasing face rather than beautiful or even pretty, a bit snub-nosed and the mouth a trifle wide, somewhat too sun-tanned to be acceptable in London society, but nice grey eyes with dark hair, simply dressed; and just on the shady side of thirty. A travelling habit like herself, past its first youth but carefully cleaned and orderly. In short, very far from the sort of trollop we had thought Haggard had fetched from London, and damnation shrewd with it too, for she glanced at him again and next inquired sweetly, "Would you be the land agent for this estate then, sir?"

That was a bit of a facer; as neat a way of asking our business as anything I could have thought of myself, and I was half at a loss before Dr Caldwell stepped in just as neatly. "Friends of the late Lord Pangersbourne, ma'am," he told her. "Particular horticultural friends, come on a sentimental journey to view what remains of the unfortunate gentleman's garden."

"*Lord* Pangersbourne?" the woman repeated. "My, sir, we had no notion that we were treading on such exalted property." She looked at Haggard again. "It seems we do trespass indeed, my dear. I'd say that we should ask pardon again, and then take ourselves off."

"Aye," he answered, though still eyeing me less than favourably, "maybe we should," while she inclined her head to us just enough to be polite, and added, "So we'll give you good day, gentlemen."

"Well," Dr Caldwell observed softly as they passed through the archway and were lost in the parkland. "Well, what do you know, Mr Sturrock? What do you make of that, sir?"

"Lying like a trooper," I announced. "And damnation saucy with it. No notion they were treading on such exalted property. They know as much about the Pangersbourne affairs as we do; very likely more."

"To be sure," he agreed, gazing after the pair of 'em thoughtfully for a minute.

He seemed about to add something else but thought better of it, turning to look about at the disorder of the garden instead, and I asked, "How do you come here so well met but unexpected, sir?"

"Simple enough," he said. "I was engaged to visit with Sir Joseph Banks for a few days, but had a message to my lodging saying that the old gentleman is indisposed and begging me to put it off for a while. So concluded to come down here and join you, for I'll own that I'm eaten up with curiosity. And what of you?" he inquired.

"Investigating," I replied. "And some uncommon thought provoking discoveries. I'll detail 'em as we go back to the village," I promised, for it was now too late to hope to keep my rendezouvs with Maggsy and Jagger—to say nothing of that other villain's having had more than time enough to reload his musket. Maggsy would reckon out quick enough that I had changed my plans, especially when he felt the call of his dinner. "Several adventures," I added. "Including a fracas last night; and a very fine gold watch. But before we go I'd be obliged if you'd walk about the garden with me for your expert opinion of several matters here."

There was little doubt of what that would be. The doctor was plainly shocked as we paced along the paths together, looking at the various beds and considering the melon pits and plant houses. "It'd break Pangersbourne's heart," he announced at last. "The last time I saw this it was as neat as any botanic enclosure; more so than some. Everything labelled and in order and not a weed in sight. They're natural enough; the damned things always thrive fastest in well cultivated soil. But the forcing pits and houses . . . I'd say they were deliberately wrecked; by several people at least, and all about the same time." He looked at me shrewdly. "Is that what you mean?"

"It's precisely my conclusion," I said. "And there's

89

one more question, Doctor. How many poisonous plants could you find here?"

He looked at me still more curious. "Hard to say unless you go through 'em all. There's several hundred different sorts here. But I can show you three off hand." He nodded to a mass of pinkish purple by one of the walls. "The common foxglove, *Digitalis*. And this one . . ." indicating a strangely hooded, sombre blue spike of flower, "monkshood or *Aconitum napellus*, otherwise known as wolfsbane. That's one of the worst. But this other runs it pretty close." He reached up to a small tree, also growing by the wall, plucked a narrow shrivelled pod and cracked it into the palm of his hand to reveal four or five little black peas, not unlike peppercrns. "Laburnum, very near as bad as aconite," he said: and then added, "It's an odd question, Mr Sturrock. Are you proposing there was something of that sort about Pangersbourne's death?"

"I don't know," I confessed. "And I never come to conclusions before I have all my facts. But I can't be persuaded that Pangersbourne died of an apoplexy brought on by the loss of one mere vegetable, or even a considerable wager. Moreover there's been mention of one Mother Gossive, an old herbalist woman, that I don't like the sound of. She'd know all about these pretty things," I said, indicating the monkshood myself. "But if there's one thing certain, it's that there was several kinds of damned uncommon mischief here last July, and I've more than a notion that the child Amelia Lydia was at the bottom of at least some part of it."

This truly startled the doctor, and I repeated, "I'll tell you more as we walk back. But first of all have you found a lodging here yet?"

"I have not," he replied. "They weren't all that

welcoming when I stopped by at the inn to inquire for you. I've a hired chaise and post-boy still waiting there in case I have to go further afield."

"You shall stay here," I promised, for I had several plans in mind already for this excellent gentleman and I liked his company. "I don't claim that I've got these damned villagers eating out of my hand just yet," I said. "But I fancy they're starting to understand that I'm not a man who can be refused anything lightly."

And so it proved. Madame Oakes was still sharp-tongued, but she had had time enough to reflect about which side her bread was buttered by now, and she admitted at length that the Widow Pinnock might be willing to accommodate the extra gentleman for a con-sideration, while if he so desired he could take his meals with us at the inn. Whereupon the occasion was more improved by the interesting discovery that the doctor had brought a basket of very fair Madeira with him. The post-boy and chaise were dismissed with instructions to look out for Jagger, Maggsy and Amelia Lydia on the road to warn them not to wait for me, and finally we all foregathered to dispose of Mrs Oakes' pair of ducks, a superior plum pie and another portion of the Dorset Blue Vinny; which was new to Dr Caldwell and much pleased him.

Then when that was finished, with further expres-sions of appreciation etc., Amelia Lydia was despatched to the kitchen where Mrs Oakes promised to teach her how to make pastry—a most useful part of any young lady's higher education—while Maggsy and Jagger, the doctor and I all retired to the stable loft with our pipes and a bottle of the Madeira. This was proposed as we were less likely to be overheard there, and we now had much to discuss, as well as receiving Maggsy's report.

91

"So let's have it," I said, when we had settled down, charged our glasses and got our pipes started.

"We got something wrong about what that Captain Haggard and his woman was up to in Romsey," he announced. "And it's uncommon rummy."

"Wait a minute," I checked him. "I thought I sent you to Wittings End to look for Dr Birdlip."

"So you did, and what we done," he retorted. "But there ain't much in that."

"Birdlip?" Dr Caldwell looked at me inquiringly.

"Do you know him then?" I asked.

"Say rather that I know of him." He nodded to Maggsy. "But let the boy continue first."

"All right then," Maggsy said. "Birdlip, for what it's worth. We go off at a spanker, and all jolly, Peggoty exclaiming and waving her ribbons to everything we pass, like she always does in the chaise, and then when we get on a bit she asks "What're we going to Wittings End for?" and I says 'To find Dr Birdlip'. Upon which she lets out a screech that damned near bolted the hosses. 'Oh no' she cries, 'not bloody likely, I ain't letting that old such-and-such pull any more of my teeth'. And nothing couldn't quieten her neither."

"Be damned," I observed. "That child's always a calamity. So what did you do?"

"What could we do? Another minute and she'd have had the chaise and all of us arse over tip. I swore we wouldn't go nowhere near Dr Birdlip, but reckoning the way you'd go on about it then told Jaggs to stop at the first inn or ale house in the place. Which he done, and which I went inside and inquired 'For God's sake where do we find Dr Birdlip, as my little sister's been took with the vapours and needs a draught', to which one of the coves there replies 'It sounds as if she needs a knock on the head, but for what good Birdlip might be he's at Garden Lodge, Badger's Lane'. And that's all there is to that."

"And not much either," I looked back at Dr Caldwell. 'But perhaps you can add something to it, sir."

"A little, although I never met the gentleman." He was most improperly amused by Maggsy, which served only to encourage the wretch. "He was Pangersbourne's physician, as you seem already to know if you are interested in him. But he was, or is, also a fellow horticulturist. Not to the same extent, I understood, yet nevertheless something of a rival. Pangersbourne told me that he has a nephew or some relative in your Navy, who sometimes brings him bundles of plants and roots. It's a not uncommon practice with ship's officers nowadays. Pangersbourne was particularly jealous of orchids which Birdlip received occasionally."

"So ho," I mused. "And our late lordship is said to have sold out a cricket match to Wittings End in consideration of some such things. The plot thickens a bit more. And the wager he had over his Venus's Fly Trap. Could that have been with Dr Birdlip, think you?"

Dr Caldwell nodded. "It's by no means unlikely."

"And Dr Birdlip would know well enough how to nobble that horrible vegetable. Whereupon his lordship dies suddenly and no questions asked. Be damned, I've never met anything like this before. It gets tastier every minute."

"It gets a lot tastier yet," Maggsy observed. "I keep trying to tell you about Romsey. You reckon that Captain Haggard and his woman went there to see where Roderick Pangersbourne and that actress was married, don't you? Well, they didn't." He leered at me evilly. They went to see where she was *buried*. And that's a trifle different, ain't it?"

93

"They did what?" I demanded, thunderstruck.

"See what I mean?" he asked Jagger; to which Jagger replied with his horse's grin, while Maggsy continued, "It was still early when we done all we could about Dr Birdlip, so I says 'We can't go back to Sturrock with no more'n that, Jaggs, so whatsay we drive on to The George at Romsey to see what we can find out there?' Which Jaggs agrees and which we done, Peggoty getting inquisitive again, and me telling her this time that we're just going to see a man about a pair of pigeons. And you recollect that when we come down the other day we stopped outside to have our drinks, while Jaggs went on his own to talk to the ostler? Well, this time we all went in."

He paused for his effect. "And as soon as I see that taproom I sees we'd found something. For it was proper plastered with play-bills. And you also recollect that one Mr Sims the theatrical agent sent you? 'Presenting a distinguished company of the most celebrated ladies and gentlemen from the Theatre Royal, Drury Lane,' Well, there it was, staring me in the chaps. So I took Jaggs aside and whispered to him 'It looks like there's something here that Sturrock wouldn't want Peggoty to know; take her for a ride and buy her a toffee apple or something". And as soon as they'd gone I says to the landlord 'I perceive you've got an interest in the Thespian profession'."

He paused again. "You never see anything like that landlord. Face as cheerful as a half starved blood hound, but otherwise most monstrous fat. Turned out as he'd been an actor himself, used to do the grave-digger in *Hamlet*, reckoned he was the finest that ever trod the boards until he got too fat for it; and, God's Whiskers, once you got him started you couldn't stop him. All of a sudden he puts one hand on his hip, seizes a quart pot in the other and holds it up above his head and declaims 'A whoreson mad fellow's it was; whose do you think it was? A pestilence on him for a mad rogue! a' poured a flagon of Rhenish on my head once. This same skull, sir, was Yorick's skull, the king's jester'. Then when he cooled down a bit he says 'My pot representing the skull; what d'you think of that?' and I says 'Fantastical; it gives you the cold grues', and my oath it did as well."

"Maggsy," I implored the monster, "for God's sake come to the meat of it," but Dr Caldwell murmured, "Let the boy tell it in his own way; I've not been so entertained in years."

Master Maggsy shot me a look of wicked triumph. "I'm coming to it. So I take another peer at that play bill and announce 'What ho, I've heard a bit of something about this one, Miss Clarissa du Frésne de Champillion; didn't she marry some lordship or the other?" And that very near set him off in a fresh rhapsody. 'Ah, the pore pretty child,' he cried. 'The pore sweet innocent', and then added 'Not that she wasn't as hard as fling with it; a right wicked little bitch.' Well, it all come out then. Seems this travelling company was a reg'lar thing, every season, and when any of 'em was down on their knockers—got no money," he explained kindly for Dr Caldwell's benefit, "which was most of the time, the landlord let 'em lodge in an old barn he'd got."

Maggsy paused yet again; not for effect now, but because for once in his life even he was troubled. "Well the landlord don't just recollect the date, which ain't surprising as it must've been thirteen years or more ago, but he remembers the occasion right enough. For they fetched Miss Clarissa and so on into the inn well gone in the apple cart, and Mrs Landlord done midwife for her. Which is nothing particular out of the way, as it might

95

happen to anybody; except that she took a fever and died of it three or four days after. And the landlord likewise remembers what was pretty near her last words. She says, 'Well, I had a try for the title and the money; I thought he'd swallow anything, but I forgot how I should have to give my name." Whatever that might mean," Maggsy finished. "And that was our Peggoty's mother."

There was a profound silence while we digested this, until I said, "You've got good wits in your head, my lad. You did well to send the child out before she heard any of that. And she never must hear any either."

"Tasty though, ain't it?" he inquired. "I reckon we should've done better to leave this lot alone. We're only stirring up the muck. Anyway, there it is. The theatricals had a whip round to bury her as decent as they could, and the end of it was that they couldn't do with the baby at the inn, as she wasn't their business, so the theatricals took her. And it must have been them that sent her to the old lord in the property basket. Come to think of it, it was the only thing they could've done."

I nodded, in profound thought. "At least it supposes they knew she was Roderick's child. The question now is whether he had married the woman or not. And that's what we still have to find out."

"Lord Pangersbourne appeared to be sure enough on that score," Dr Caldwell observed. "I think I told you at our first meeting that he presented her as his granddaughter."

"He couldn't very well do anything else, could he?" I asked. "And seeing the way some of these actresses carry on, and in particular this one by the sound of it, let's hope he was right. I fancy there's more property than we yet know of concerned, and plainly other people sniffing about after it. If there's any doubt we shall have the devil's own convocation of lawyers to contend with before we've done."

"D'you mean to say you're going on?" Maggsy demanded.

"I mean to see that Amelia Lydia's better treated in the future than she has been in the past. So let's now continue with your report. Did you learn any more about Captain Haggard and the woman?"

"Not a lot." He appeared to be somewhat indifferent. "I let on they was friends of mine and got mislaid, but the landlord wasn't all that interested. Seems true that they took the cheapest room in the place—not that I'd have thought there was all that much choice—though the woman had it to herself, for the captain slept on a bench in the tap." He sniffed. "Most uncommon respectable."

"So he also saw that play-bill," I said.

"Couldn't have missed it. I inquired did they ask any questions about it, as I let on they was theatricals themselves, and the landlord says he wouldn't have thought so, but they didn't. The only other thing was that when they was having their supper he heard the captain say something to the effect that if it was the same families they was old friends, and bound to remember him, and they was pretty well sure to be, as they always worked the same round. Then as they was going off the next morning the woman said 'That's one errand I'll not come on with you; I'll go to take the air and look at the market while you're about it'. And that's all," Maggsy finished. "So what did you find up at the house?"

"It was what I didn't find that most aroused my interest," I said, but before I could get any further Jagger muttered, "Hold your hosses, guv'nor," and crept across the loft in his stockinged feet. The rascal always throws his boots off when sitting at ease, much to

97

everybody else's discomfort, and nothing I can ever say or do will break him of the habit, but on this occasion it served him well, for he went as soft as a cat. "Keep talking," he whispered over his shoulder, somewhat contradictory, and I continued, "But I brought some papers away out of curiosity . . ." just as he flung open the door at the top of the stairs to a most blood-curdling yell. Then followed a fresh screech and Jagger rolled down the stairs with another body clasped in his arms. They damned near shook the entire place apart between 'em, landed with a crash and chorus of howls and curses that set the horses kicking in their stalls, and for some time nothing could be seen but a perfect storm of hay, straw and dust flying about everywhere below.

What with Jagger giving tongue, whatever else it was down there screeching, two or three hens squawking about shedding feathers everywhere and Master Maggsy adding his own unlovely observations to the uproar, it was near enough a witch's hornpipe until I cried, "Be damned, Jagger, stop that, you rascal." Then at last the cloud subsided, Dr Caldwell again unseasonably amused, remarking something about the peace of quiet English country life, Jagger revealed trying to brush off a fowl that was perching on his head, and clutching by the hair the horrid small stable-boy whom he addressed affectionately as Pig's Arse. "Little bugger," he announced. "Eavesdropping on us."

"So ho," said I, descending the stairs myself, with Dr Caldwell and Maggsy behind me, all of us surveying the filthy wretch. "And who set you on to that?" I asked kindly.

"Mind your bliddy own business,' he replied with the natural courtesy of these villagers, at the same time aiming a vicious kick at Jagger's shins, while Maggsy inquired, "He's a good game 'un, ain't he?"

"He's a little viper," Jagger anounced, giving him another clout to calm him, but fetching a fresh screech and a flow of poetics surprising in one so young and innocent.

"You want to watch out," he roared. "Us knows what to do with nosey sods like 'ee. They'll have 'ee in the mill pond as well before you've done ef you ain't careful."

"Wait," I told Jagger as he was about to admonish the creature further, for in a sudden flash I perceived what had happened here a twelvemonth back, how Thomas Grubbage had died, and why. "Let him be, Jagger," I said, and continued, "Come, my lad, speak up and don't be afraid. They make a habit of it here, do they? Ducking people in the mill pool if they have a disagreement with 'em?"

"You'll find out soon enough," he screeched again. "Tek a look out there. They're waiting for 'ee now. Just tek a look," he repeated evilly, and Maggsy scurried across to the half door.

We could now hear the growl of voices as he opened the top part a crack, and a damned ugly growl. One of them bawled, "What be they doing of to 'ee in there, Jemmy?" and Maggsy turned back to us with a face like a spavined codfish. "We got trouble," he announced simply.

SIX

It was an ugly situation; ten or twelve of the villagers grouped in a half circle about the stable door, not a few of them bearing muck-forks and other unfavourable implements, and all looking ready to pick a quarrel. Most of the rabble that was in the tap last night, Moses and Aaron in their smocks but otherwise like Biblical prophets waiting for doom, a few women at cottage doors with several urchins, and the rascal Smallbrook hanging back but alight with mischief; and I would have offered better than evens that he was the rascal out with a fowling-piece this morning. "So how do we get out of this?" Maggsy chattered behind me, while Dr Caldwell, still with some amusement and the coolest possible manner, observed, "Here's a rail-riding party, I guess; I've seen the Orinoco Indians looking friendlier."

But if the doctor was cool, so was I. When you've seen the worst the Seven Dials can do you can't be daunted by a mere country mob. "Show 'em a touch of authority," said I, as they muttered among themselves. "Well now," I addressed them, "what's this? A deputation, is it? Come to ask my coachman to play for you on Saturday?" That struck 'em with surprise for a minute, and I opened the lower half of the door and stepped outside, adding, "Speak up one of you. I daresay he'll oblige if you ask him polite enough."

"God's sake, watch it," Maggsy muttered, and on the same instant two or three fowls and the little wretch Pig's Arse all came flying out, all clucking, squawking and squealing together. I damned near went down in the rush had not Dr Caldwell caught at my arm, but the incident fetched a jeering laugh which changed to a wicked growl as the dreadful child screeched, "Plotting and scheming, they was; and very near killed me."

That might have started the rush there and then but for Mrs Oakes, who now appeared at the inn door bearing a slopping pail of water, and screaming, "Git back inside, yer bliddy fules, there'll be murder done!" So saying she flung the water first and the pail after it, bellowed, "Fetch the bliddy pa'son, somebody!" kilted up her skirts and set off at a gallop across the green herself. It steadied them that got the dousing, and while they was wondering about it in their country manner Dr Caldwell held up his one hand, stuck the thumb of the other in his weskit pocket and addressed them in terms of such pure Massachusetts that they seemed struck dumb for a minute. I would never have believed it from an academic botanical gentleman.

"Well spoken, sir," said I, and it fetched a better-humoured laugh not without a certain admiration, but there were some here who were bent on mischief at any cost, for one of 'em safely at the back bawled, "Run 'em out with a fork to their arses," and Master Smallbrook yelled, "Have 'em in the mill pond." They who were closer to me and Dr Caldwell however was less eager, and with a fine careless manner, staring 'em out now with both thumbs stuck in the armholes of his weskit, the doctor said amiably, "Make way there, gentlemen," while not to be outdone I added, " '*Odi profanum vulgus et arceo*'; I hate the vulgar throng and drive them from me; Horace."

That also had 'em puzzled for a minute, and all might still have been well if Miss Amelia Lydia had not chosen to show herself at the inn door and screech some rude observation, whereat several of the horrid children promptly screeched back, started flinging a perfect hail of stones, and the battle started. One rascal made a pass at me with a dung-fork, and Dr Caldwell floored him with as neat a snouter as I have ever seen; I performed the like service for the doctor as another made a wicked rush at him with a cudgel; Maggsy and Jagger came roaring out with further forks they had discovered in the stable. In short it was a battle royal; Jagger and Maggsy fencing with these unpleasant weapons; the doctor and me fighting side by side with no holds barred; various of the women now also flinging pails of water about with wanton carelessness; and all in an uproar that could have been heard as far away as Wittings End.

But we were being beat by weight of numbers. As fast as you put one rogue down another sprang up to take his place, and these clodhoppers seemed to have harder skulls than the like sort of rascals in London. Dr Caldwell generously accounted for three or four, I for several others; Maggsy and Jagger pinked a fair selection; but we were all getting more than breathless when a mighty pulpit voice bellowed, "Blockheads; dunderheads; muttonheads; stop it; stop it, I tell you!'

And they stopped. The parson appeared striking right and left with a riding-crop, cutting his way through 'em like a black ninety-gun battleship; but his face red with fury, and his language a credit to the hunting field. "Be damned to you all," he roared, "get

102

to your homes. I shall have something to say about this."

"Then best say it now, sir," Dr Caldwell suggested. 'And in similar terms. I'd admire to hear it."

But they was all drawing away, even the women and horrible children, and Mrs Oakes was coming back to scold Amelia Lydia inside the inn again. That reverend had a more than ordinary power over these people, and a more than ordinary fear, I suspected; though only a man of my perception could have seen it. Nevertheless, he was just as brusque with us. He started, "And as for you gentlemen . . ." stopped as if he was at a loss for words and looked hard at Dr Caldwell, announced, "I've seen you here before, sir; visiting the late Lord Pangersbourne," and finally added to me, "And I should tell you, Mr Sturrock, that I know who and what you are. There was a mention of you in *The Times* newspaper recently."

"Such is the penalty of fame," I said. "But if you know who I am it saves me telling you myself; and it gives me the right to ask certain questions."

"What questions?" he demanded. "And what right? What is your business here?"

"Sir," I said, "you can refuse to answer anything and even to listen to me. But if you do I shall come to certain unfortunate conclusions. Or on the other hand we might have a quiet and private conversation with profit to all parties." I nodded at the stable door. "And there's as private as anywhere, for it's plain this village is all eyes and ears."

He could have walked away then, and was half tempted to, but he knew as well as I did that he was on the horns of a dilemma. He marched inside with a snort like a horse down his handsome canonical nose, and I continued, "It's just as plain you're protecting your parishioners, Mr Hangbolt, and that's a fine and worthy thing in a vicar: moreover it keeps the rascals in order. But it might be unwise to take it too far."

"Come to the point, sir," he rapped out. "What are you getting at?"

"Murder, sir," I said. "Of Thomas Grubbage, head gardener to the late Lord Pangersbourne, on the 11th of July last, three days after Lord Pangersbourne's own sudden death. I don't know how far several or more people might be charged with collective murder— that'd be a nice thing for the lawyers to chew over—but it's very certain that anybody knowing of the matter and wilfully concealing, obfuscating or ignoring it could be charged as accessory after the fact."

It took him clean on the waterline, but he still came back fighting. "That is arrant nonsense, sir. I don't understand a word of it."

"Then I'll explain," I said. "And to start with, there's reason to suppose that Lord Pangersbourne was more than unpopular here. He was a man of eccentric interests; and there was the matter of a cricket match against Wittings End."

"What d'you know about that?" the parson demanded, but I did not enlighten him, and he announced, "In brief, he sold the game."

"Precisely. For a mere matter of an orchid or two. It was very near as bad as the fellow who sold his birthright for a mess of pottage. But more recently he had been cultivating another outlandish vegetable; and the most alarming tales were circulating." I turned to Dr Caldwell. "Would you say that such tales could well be believed by simple, superstitious people?"

He had no doubt of it. "To the credulous all things are credible. You'd be surprised at the powers the Orinoco Indians attribute to some of their forest plants."

"And by the way they carry on these people here ain't so very far removed from wild Indians," I observed. "But mark the sad and fearful thing. It was little Amelia Lydia who first put about these tales. And Thomas Grubbage started them. For being nervous of an unruly child in his plant house, as any gardener might be, he told her that this uncommon thing—the like of which nobody had seen or heard of before—would catch her and eat her if she interfered with it. Would you also agree a fanciful child could believe that too?' I asked the doctor again.

"She wouldn't need to be all that fanciful. The plant has a trap at the end of each leaf," the doctor explained. "As it were, the palms of two hands fringed with hooks; when a fly or other insect walks between these two palms they close together in an instant. Let anybody be persuaded that it could grow big enough, and the rest needs no imagining."

"It was an ungodly thing to cultivate," Parson Hangbolt burst out. "I told Pangersbourne so. And spoke about it from the pulpit."

I regarded him thoughtfully. "Aye; I can understand you would. And thus stirred the pot a bit more. So there we have the matter; or a part of it. Grubbage told Amelia Lydia the plant would eat her. Amelia Lydia threatened she would set it on to one of the village children. And also, I fancy, told the tale to the herb woman Mother Gossive. Who very likely embroidered it still more."

I paused for the parson to answer, but seemingly he had nothing to say, and I continued, "So now we come to the devilment. The plant itself was destroyed by some hand at present unknown on or before July eight last year. On that day also Lord Pangersbourne died suddenly and unexpected. And on July eleven the mob from this village, the same mob that we had about us here, marched on Pangersbourne House in a body. It's a minor curiosity that they waited for three days,' I observed to the doctor aside. "But they set to work about the garden and plant houses while the other servants fled in a hurry. The late revolution in France has still got a lot to answer for, putting ideas into simple folk's heads. They carried off Thomas Grubbage to drive him out of the parish. And tossed him into the mill pool for a start; to speed him on his way. But they tossed him too far and too deep; and it don't take a man long to drown if nobody tries to save him."

"God's weskit," said Maggsy, who up to this had kept strangely silent. "So that's what you mean; collective murder. I never heard of it before."

"Do not blaspheme in my presence, boy," Parson Hangbolt thundered at him; and for once in a lifetime I saw Maggsy blench. But the parson continued, "This is a tarradiddle of fancy, sir. The man was drunk. That was testified at the inquest. The verdict was death by misadventure. The only decent and kindly verdict possible, as it permitted him Christian burial."

"So ho," I mused. "So there was an inquest? And who was the coroner, pray?"

"Who should it be?" he demanded. "Dr Birdlip of Wittings End."

"Dr Birdlip?" I repeated, and then stopped short myself, looking first at Maggsy and Jagger and then at Dr Caldwell lest they should make some inadvertent remark. "Well that should dispose of the matter nice enough," I observed, putting on my mildest tones. "It seems I must be mistaken. But bear with me another minute," I begged him, "for I'm bound to ask the question. Did you witness the incident yourself?"

106

"I did not," he answered shortly. "I was absent in Salisbury about church business on that day."

And that's why they waited until then, I mused; so that the parson should be out of the way. But he was growing irritable; and at the same time increasingly uneasy, I suspected; as if afraid there was more I might start getting at. "Does this improper catechism go much further?" he demanded.

"Catechism?" I cried. "Improper? Why, sir, I wouldn't dare to catechise a reverend gentleman in his own parish. I hope I've more consideration for the Cloth. But I'm a blundering, dunderheaded sort of fellow, and a thought too inquisitive at times. It was the headstone in your churchyard that set me wondering. It seems a handsome monument and epitaph to a mere gardener."

But Dr Caldwell took exception to this. "A mere gardener? Come, no gardener's ever *mere*. A good gardener's entitled to the greatest respect."

"Exactly so." It struck me that the parson clutched at that like a straw. "The villagers themselves subscribed for the stone."

"And it's a credit to their nicer feelings," I observed warmly. "Was it their own idea?"

"At my behest," he said, short again.

So he knew precisely what had happened; and he was a man of justice in his way, I reflected. That stone was a penance and reminder to the rascals; though it might hang somebody yet if I chose to push it so far. But I finished, "Well, there it is, sir. Whatever was done a twelvemonth since can't be undone now, and there's no thought of subjecting you to a catechism. Yet you'll own we've a right to be a bit perturbed when these folk set about us for no good reason. It's bound to start us thinking that they've got something to hide. And that's

107

not all of it, either. There was somebody uncommon careless with a fowling-piece damnation close by my head this morning."

"What?" he demanded, startled again. "Where was this?"

"Up at the house. When Dr Caldwell and I were studying the damage to the garden there."

I fancy he muttered something strangely uncanonical under his breath, but he said, "Poaching. You can't stop 'em. And with no known owner to the property at present they regard anything in the coverts and park as fair game for the pot. Nevertheless I'll have a sharp word about it."

"We shall be profoundly obliged," I assured him. "We don't like ill feeling, nor people shooting at us, for there's no need of it; and we don't want to leave before your cricket match on Saturday; which we're much looking forward to. And as to that," I asked, "have you had any word of your blacksmith, Ironband, yet?"

"We haven't." He gave me a long hard look as if he suspected that we were somehow at the bottom of the fellow's absence. "It's causing some concern. We shall make a weaker team if anything's happened to him; to say nothing of one of my horses missing. And Mrs Ironband also is becoming alarmed."

"A serious situation," I observed. "Have you made any inquiry?" He seemed as if he was about to tell me to mind my own business, but thought better. "I despatched his apprentice to Ringwood this morning. But we can hardly expect him back before nightfall."

"And apprentices never hurry themselves. Well now," I proposed, "since you've discovered that I'm the first officer of Bow Street, why don't you call us in to investigate?" Both Maggsy and Jagger looked at me, scenting fresh work, but if it were possible the parson was more suspicious than ever.

"I hardly think Ironband's worthy of your talents," he said. "He's very likely merely fallen prey to his difficulties again. And if you'll give me leave now, I've other matters to attend to."

"Give you leave, sir?" I cried. "I wouldn't presume so much. It's a kindness on your part to have spared us so much of your time. But we've heard of Ironband's troubles and difficulties from other people. Pray tell me, what are they?"

The parson hesitated, and then replied briefly, "Drink. He was a sober fellow at one time, until he returned here wounded from the army . . ." He stopped on that as if catching himself up from saying too much. "Ironband will go for months without touching a drop," he finished as he turned away. "But once let something start him and he may be incapable for days on end."

"So ho," said I, watching the reverend gentleman march across the green. "So Ironband was in the army, and now he's merely lying drunk somewhere. What did you make of all that, sir?" I asked the doctor.

He gave a dry little chuckle. "Why, that your parson's a righteous man in his own fashion, and leaving much unspoken. It seemed to me that he was half expecting you to go on to something else beside Thomas Grubbage and the blacksmith."

"And was plainly relieved that I didn't," I finished. "Be damned, the more you uncover in this place, the more there seems to be beneath it. But let's go to see what Mrs Oakes has got for our supper; if she's not so much out of temper that she's forgot all about it."

But she was that rare jewel of a woman who does not let such small things as riot and murder interfere with her cooking. She gave us a dish of sweet little trout—once again no doubt poached—and a simple but honest capon, while Dr Caldwell kept Miss Amelia Lydia quiet and Maggsy and Jagger goggle-eyed by recounting some of his experiences in the Orinoco forests. But when that was done, and Mrs Oakes came in to carry of the remnants, she sent the child out to the kitchen to bring in the apple pie, and asked bluntly, "Well then, how much d'you know?"

"Pretty near everything," I answered; which was not precisely the truth; but close enough to be useful.

She pondered that for a minute like a mountain in thought. "And what d'ye mean to do about it?"

"Nothing," I told her. 'Not unless something's forced on us. But any more jostling or frolicking with muskets or other weapons might upset me."

It was plain that we understood each other, for she nodded. "Aye. They're a pack of fules; as idle and shiftless as most men everywhere. But I'll see that some get a bit of sense talked into 'em, though I wish to God none of us had ever set eyes on you. And I'll tell you for the last time, the sooner you get that child out of here the better."

"Now why, Mrs Oakes?" I inquired. "Apart from starting the riot last year, and that all unwitting, what harm can she do now?"

"Children's tongues wag mischievous sometimes," she observed. "And there's some have cause to fear that hers might wag too much. I'll say no more than that."

"So what might that mean, I wonder?" Maggsy asked softly as the good woman left us, and I said, "It's plain enough; and you know what to do. When we've finished our supper you and Jagger can play a game of cards with Amelia Lydia to keep her amused. And with your approval, sir," I proposed to Dr Caldwell, "we'll

110

adjourn to my room to see what else we can put together between us."

"The girl knows something, think you?" he asked, when we had settled there, opened another bottle of his excellent Madeira and filled our pipes.

"It's very likely," I said. "And may not be aware of what it is or what it means herself. She might have let something slip that Mrs Oakes sees the significance of. Whichever way it is children are the devil and damnation to get anything certain out of, for you're never sure you can believe a word the little monsters say. But she'll chatter like a magpie to Maggsy and Jagger."

I listened to the conversation down in the taproom for a minute, but there was no more than half a dozen in there and all somewhat subdued. Aaron and Moses were doing their recitative and response, the others muttering about the absence of blacksmith Ironband, and I observed, "That's certainly a matter we shall have to look into tomorrow; but for now, Dr Caldwell, I've a curious little question for you." I went on to tell him about the entries in Lord Pangersbourne's horticultural diaries, his subscriptions to the various expeditions, etc., and then inquired. "Will you tell me, when he paid the two hundred guineas towards yours, did he issue an order on his bank or hand you the funds in cash?"

"Why, there's an oddity," said the doctor, "and odder still that you should ask. He paid in cash; in gold, and a rare mixed lot. There were even George Second pieces among it. To tell the truth it was tarnation inconvenient, as nobody likes to carry that amount of coinage about in his baggage in a civilised country, and I don't have my own bank here. I had to get one of the other gentlemen of the Horticultural Society—Mr Wedg-

111

wood—to deposit it to his account and then issue an order on that. I recollect that Wedgwood said it was a habit of Pangersbourne's. And he'd done the same on an earlier occasion when I was visiting here; though for a smaller amount then."

"And if I might presume to ask still further, had you had any previous dealings with him?"

"One other; the first. I was in Boston at that time, planning an exploration along the Louisiana St Francis River, and the arrangement was by introduction and correspondence."

"And the subscription then was made by order and banker's transfer?"

"That was the only way it could have been made." He was growing puzzled. "Does this mean anything, Mr Sturrock?"

"It might do. I have a nose for these things, and I seem to smell something here. As you say, an oddity. It comes back to whether he was insolvent or not at the time of his death, and I would say he most certainly was not. In November of 1814 he subscribed another hundred to a James Hunter in Philadelphia; also by order. And among his papers there is a letter from this gentleman acknowledging receipt in March of the following year."

"I knew of that. In fact I recommended Hunter to him. A very good man. Gets on famously with the Delaware Indians, and speaks their language as he might have been born to it. He works west of the Missouri, following the trail of the Lewis and Clark expedition to the Pacific Coast in 1803. Pangersbourne was already growing some of the Lewisias discovered on that exploration." The doctor stopped short at that, gazing at me over his glass of Madeira. "Come to think of it I didn't see them in the garden this morning. I

112

wonder where they got to? They're not the easiest things to cultivate, and Pangersbourne and Grubbage were uncommonly successful; and proud of them."

To tell the truth all this was beyond me, for I am never ashamed to admit ignorance on the rare occasions that I suffer from it. I said politely, "You'll know more about that side of it than I can pretend to, sir. What I'm coming to is that his lordship seems to have preferred to subscribe in cash whenever it was possible. And there's a letter also among his papers which would appear to suggest that he kept a small special balance for the occasions when he was obliged to issue an order."

Dr Caldwell looked at me keenly again. "Meaning what?"

"I don't know yet," I confessed. "But here's another oddity. I said I was more interested in what I didn't find. There was no sign of any other accounts, rent rolls, agents' or lawyers' correspondence, or estate balance."

He refilled our glasses. "And the room had already been searched."

"At least once before. And very thoroughly."

"The Virginia title deeds?" the doctor suggested.

"With all respect, I doubt it," I said. "I doubt that anybody in this place would have much interest in those, even if they remain valid. In my opinion we've a mystery here that hangs on one or another of his lordship's eccentricities. I wish I'd had time to study those day to day books of his more closely; and we might have to yet, though I fancy they'll mean more to you than to me. But I brought away several other documents. I hardly know why, except that they struck me as curious."

So saying I took out the South Sea Company bonds and the map of the estate, and we fell to studying them between us, the doctor by the nature of his interests

113

being more attentive to the map. "A nice hand with cartography, that William Hawkins," he mused. "And a considerable property at this date, 1714. The village and water-mill, and eight farms," he said, counting them up. "And these marked off and crossed in red; five of them with further dates; 1721 and '22. What do those indicate, I wonder? Do you think the same as I do, sir?"

"It's quite plain," I agreed. "Those farms were sold off. And that would be about the time of the late Lord Pangersbourne's grandfather."

"Near enough a hundred years ago. Does it mean much to us now?" he asked.

"I'm convinced it does. Not least because it still leaves a very comfortable property which should come to the child. But my instinct tells me that somewhere in it, and in these things, there's a thread to our present mystery." I turned over the bond certificates to add up the figures on them and was very near dumbfounded by the total. "There was five thousand here. And waste paper now. For what it may be worth these things at least tell why those farms were sold. The Pangersbourne of that time got his fingers burned, not to say his eyebrows singed and his hair scorched off in the South Sea Bubble."

"I fear you have me there, sir," the gentleman observed mildly, and just for once in a while I was thankful for my own chance of explaining something he didn't seem to know.

"A speculation mania and financial disaster that ruined thousands in this country. A joint-stock company formed in 1711 and granted the monopoly of trade with the Spanish Americas. In 1720 it made an offer to take over and convert the National Debt in return for a total monopoly of the South Seas trade, and gambling went mad. Everybody who could raise the

114

price of a few shares ran wild to buy 'em. There were vendors at the very street corners in the City of London. In June of that year the shares stood at a hundred and twenty-five above par, by August they had shot up to a thousand, and by September they weren't worth the paper they were printed on. A few made fortunes out of it, but most lost everything they'd got. The entire country was damned close to bankruptcy that autumn, ministers said to be up to their snouts in corruption, and local banks closing everywhere. And they who didn't lose their money when the bubble burst lost it as the banks failed."

"It's a wonder it didn't cause a revolution," Dr Caldwell observed.

I looked at him sharply, for even the most genteel of Americans sometimes have strange notions in that direction. "It very near did; except for the Walpole administration. But let's stick to the Pangersbournes. By the look of it they bought in when the shares were already standing high, and they lost the half of their property through 'em. Maybe more if they sold off other assets."

"Seemingly not as bad as most people then. Though still enough to make any family careful in future. But so long ago, Mr Sturrock." He shook his head. "I still don't see how it may touch our present problem."

"No more do I. Yet I say again the thread's there if only we can pick it up. And I'll wager that parson might tell us a good deal about it."

"And he knows you're an officer of Bow Street. And you know the truth about the Grubbage affair. Don't that give you a power to question him?"

"I've no authority and no proof. And it'd take a month of Sundays to get either. There was an inquest and verdict on Grubbage, improper as it must have been. Parson Hangbolt could advise me to take myself to the devil, and there's little doubt that he would. No, sir; we've got to get a tighter hold on him than that. In the meantime we can only hope that the answer to any one of our questions may throw some light on the others. God knows we've a wide choice. What is somebody searching for here? Is it that or something Amelia Lydia knows, or has seen or heard, which might put her in danger? What is it that worries Parson Hangbolt as much as the untimely end of Thomas Grubbage? Who is Captain Haggard, what is he after and who is the woman with him? And I can think of several more concerning the servants at the house, the other gardeners, Mother Gossive, etc."

"As to the woman . . ." The doctor paused to refill his pipe and recharge our glasses. "I guess I've been holding out a mite, but I wanted to think the matter over first before speaking of it. I'd say she fits pretty well with that watch you were telling me you took from the gipsy last night. Made by Frémont of Richmond, and inscribed 'H. G. de Bourne'."

"It's a gentleman's timepiece," I said, taking it out to show him again.

"I don't see that signifies much." He turned it over in his fingers and opened the case. "It's a traveller's watch; and a rare nice piece. Well now," he inquired, "did ye note the habit the woman was wearing when she appeared today? And the softish drawl in her speech? Those clothes were American-made, Mr Sturrock. I know the cut of our tailoring when I see it, much as the ladies like to model their dress on the Parisian fashions. And I know the speech. That young woman is a Virginian born and bred, sir."

"A fine travelling timepiece made in America and American-cut clothes," I mused. "So we're back to the

116

Virginia title deeds again."

"I'd say it's very likely. And back to an American branch of the Pangersbourne family. Recollect that those deeds were in the name of an Isaac Bourne, wool merchant of London and Chipping Campden."

"Be damned," I observed, "it confuses more than it solves. The fellow who calls himself Captain Hagard is as English as I am. And how does the watch come to be in the possession of that gipsy rascal?"

Dr Caldwell chuckled. "I've known Indians who could steal the tobacco out of your pipe while you're still smoking it; and gipsies are not unlike. For the rest I'd say we shall get the answers easiest by finding these people and asking them."

"Precisely so, sir," I replied, somewhat nettled at being taught my own business. "And along with several other matters that's an exercise for tomorrow." But before I could elaborate further Master Maggsy announced his presence by a clumping of fairy feet on the stairs, and I asked the question which was now becoming a kind of password with us. "Where's the child?"

"Kitchen again," he answered briefly. "Played cards with us a bit, took sixpence off me and a shilling of Jagger, the little sharper, and then Mrs Battleship come in to fetch her to help with the washing-up; an not before time neither, or she'd have skinned us. Jagger's gone into the tap to have a pint or two and see whether any of 'em fancies to pick another bone with him."

"Then he should have had more sense," I observed, listening for a minute. But all seemed quiet enough down there, and I asked, "Did you learn anything new from her?"

"Heard it all before one time and one way and another, ain't we? It's a matter of putting all of her

117

multitudinous several tales arse about face and sideways to end to see which way they make sense," he explained to Dr Caldwell. "She ain't exactly a little liar but she gets took with fits of fancy. Anyway there was something a bit different this time. So far as I can make out it was this Mother Gossive who took her to the gipsies."

"So ho," I said, "that mysterious old woman again. Let's have it."

"I'm telling you, ain't I?" he asked. "Seems like she was in some sort of trouble with the old lord having seen him about something she shouldn't have seen; as we know she's inquisitive and nosey. Well then the old lord sent for the housekeeper, Mrs Coggins, and told her to take Peggoty away and lock her up in her own room until she learned to mind her own business; which Mrs Coggins done. And Peggoty knows that was a Saturday, as next day when it happened the church bells was ringing."

"For God's sake," I demanded, "when what happened?"

"When the old lord dropped down dead. Like I said, it was the morning and the church bells was ringing and all of a sudden there was a perfect uproar, and everybody screeching and hooting, and after a time Mrs Coggins comes to her and says his lordship's dropped dead in the plant house and a most fearful sight, being black in the face and foaming at the mouth and horrible sick, and she wasn't to go nowhere near him. Which Peggoty don't want to and couldn't anyway, as they locked her in again. Next come the parson, and tells her that his lordship has passed away, the same being sad, but a judgement on him; and she's a poor child of calamity and she'll have to go to an orphan's home."

He stopped for breath, and then continued, "So that night she slept with Mrs Coggins to keep the abdabs away from both of 'em, and the day following—that being the Monday—who should come but Mother Gossive. And she says Peggoty'll be better off with the gipsies, as there'd very likely be mischief done before long; which Peggoty reckoned she would also as she wasn't going to let the parson send her to no home of no sort."

Dr Caldwell looked at Maggsy consideringly. "It's a strange story. And remarkably clear for a child of that age, and twelve months ago."

"That's me," Maggsy said modestly. "I put it together straight. Like I said, you always have to take Peggoty's tales as they come and sort 'em out, but I think most of that's the truth. Me and Jaggs've heard bits of it before, but never all together to believe it. And there was something about peppercorns as well, this time."

"Peppercorns?" I repeated sharply. "What about peppercorns?"

"Dunno." The wretch seemed indifferent again. "Never asked her. Once I'd got her started on one tale I didn't want to turn her off on another, but it was something else to do with Mother Gossive."

The doctor now looked at me just as inquiring, plainly thinking of the question I had asked him in the garden that morning, and I answered, "Quite so, sir. And the more we uncover the less I like what we find."

"Told you so didn't I?" Maggsy observed. "I told you we was only stirring up the muck; though I don't see what peppercorns've got to do with it. But I'll ask her if you like."

"No," I said. "Not on any account. We must get to the bottom of it some other way. First of all tomorrow, Dr Birdlip the coroner; and if he's like one or two other coroners I've met it might well be a stormy meeting.

119

And in the meantime, Dr Caldwell, your acumen and assistance. You're to lodge with the Widow Pinnock tonight, and widow women are notorious gossips with kindly gentlemen. I'll not be so bold as to advise you, sir. In short, anything you may glean. Those days last July; Mother Gossive; the gipsies and tinkers; and not least the man Smallbrook. But no more questions to the child," I told Maggsy. "Not unless or until we're forced to ask 'em. The last thing we ever want her to learn is that she might have had a hand in poisoning her own grandfather."

SEVEN

Before retiring to our beds we made all our arrangements for tomorrow, and pretty well at first light—or at least before the village was astir, which was quite early enough—Maggsy and Jagger crept down from their stable loft, while I descended from my own scarcely more commodious chamber, to meet Dr Caldwell at the churchyard gate and then go on straight and quick to Pangersbourne House. Needless to say my two fine fellows complained bitterly of the untimely hour with nothing on their stomachs, but I told them briskly that we didn't need any prying eyes after us or another careless rascal with a fowling-piece again.

"Moreover we've a long and busy day before us," I said. "For I can see now what might put the calamity child in danger and several other matters, and I mean to get to the bottom of this ugly affair as quick as we can now. To that end did you learn anything from the Widow Pinnock?" I asked the doctor.

"A little," he replied. "And perhaps significant. I invited her to a glass or two of the Madeira, which made her sufficiently loquacious. The housekeeper, Mrs Coggins—in fact she appears to have been the cook—was an old friend and gossip of hers, and had been with

Pangersbourne for many years; a woman from Dorchester, and she returned there some time shortly after his death. His lordship kept a reduced establishment and the other servants were mere silly girls who seemingly also departed. The Venus's Fly Trap he was cultivating was certainly an object of terror in the village."

I was a trifle impatient. "With respect, sir, we already know or surmise that much."

"Quite so," he agreed imperturbably. "It grows more interesting, however. According to Mrs Coggins Pangersbourne was addicted to highly spiced foods, which she said inflamed his stomach and frequently made him exceedingly irritable."

"So ho," I said. "Now we begin to learn something. That Madeira you brought is a most excellent vintage. Did she speak of the man Smallbrook and Mother Gossive?"

"Considerably; after some prompting; and to particular interest." He paused aggravatingly to survey the summer early-morning mist rising from the meadows beyond the church. "There are three main families of gipsies who by long tradition come to the same close by encampment every July, August and September. They are the Abels, the Tickners, and the Smallbrooks. And this village Smallbrook is the illegitimate son of the woman Gossive or Godsave by one of the gipsy men of that name."

Still more impatient I observed, "It's an old country custom, sir; they don't have any other amusement in the long dark nights," but the gentleman went on at his own precise pace.

"No doubt. But here we come to the heart of the matter. Pangersbourne was curiously tolerant of the old woman for her herbal knowledge and her botanical interest. He permitted her in his garden whenever she chose to come and allowed her the free tenancy of a bothy or hovel in the thicket by the water-mill; and, although the son was known as an inveterate poacher and horse-thief with the forest ponies you have here, Pangers-bourne showed him the same tolerance. Yet . . ."

The man stopped for another of his damnation pauses, and then continued, "Here our good widow was becoming tarnation confused but garrulous, for she had taken to that Madeira like a duck to water. In brief, she was by no means clear when this occurred; but as far as I could understand it was not more than a day or so before Pangersbourne's death. Mrs Coggins and several other servants heard and observed Pangersbourne and Thomas Grubbage engaged about a violent altercation with Smallbrook in the garden. Grubbage was flourish-ing a spade and threatening he would kill him. Pangers-bourne was saying words to the effect "I'll give you all the botany you want, you villain, for I'll see you deported to Botany Bay for it; and I'll have that damned old mother of yours turned off my land to starve'. By this time Widow Pinnock was finding her tongue a mite uncertain," the doctor finished mildly. "As instance she pronounced 'botany' as 'borr'ny', but she understood the reference to Botany Bay clearly enough. There is no doubt that that is what Mrs Coggins related to her; and very little of what is means."

"Very little," I agreed. "It means Smallbrook nobbled that damned vegetable, and we may not have far to look to find who set him on to it. Clearly Grubbage or his lordship discovered the fact, and if he was threat-ening to have Smallbrook brought up and deported, and the mother turned out—as in both cases he could have done—there we have the motive for murder."

"It gets real tasty, don't it?" Maggsy announced. "But what's our Peggoty got to do with it?"

123

"I suspect they used her to introduce the poison, may God forgive them. I don't see how it could have been done otherwise. Did the widow disclose anything else?" I asked Dr Caldwell.

He shook his head, "Not to any account. But I fancied that, like your parson, there was something she expected me to ask and was relieved when I didn't."

"And I've more than a notion I know what that is too. That's something more we'll have out with the Reverend Hangbolt before we've done today," I promised.

"Then I wish I knowed as well," the good simple Jagger complained. "And I wish I knowed why we're thumping about here at this time of the morning without our breakfasts."

"We're looking for a peppermill," I said.

"It's merely to satisfy myself," I explained to Dr Caldwell as we entered the house from the kitchen yard, having posted Maggsy to keep watch at the front and Jagger in the stables at the back. "For unless we can wring a confession out of the rascal we shall never get at the whole truth," I said. "And even if we do I should hesitate to bring him to trial. My blood runs cold at the thought of what any lawyer might twist that child into saying before a judge and jury."

"I begin to suspect you have a fondness for her," he observed drily. "As I confess I have. And I fancy she's smart enough to be a match for most of 'em."

"She's a natural calamity," I declared, while we stood for a minute to survey the first kitchen. "And that's how she'd appear in court. We must settle this ourselves somehow; so let's set about it, for we've little time to waste."

To confess the truth I more than half feared that we

124

were wasting it anyway. Anything could have happened in a twelvemonth, and it was a dismal business in the dank silence and dim light, poking about in the unsavoury disorder left by those wretched servants when they fled. Smallbrook might have got into the house to purloin the peppermill and remove the evidence. But I had an obstinate notion that that was not within the rascal's character. It was too open and bold. He would count the risk of that greater than the chance of anybody ever seeing the trick, not expecting the wit of Jeremy Sturrock and the obscure retribution of the Lord to get after him in the end.

And my instinct was proved correct, as it almost always is; for we found the object after a brief search in the silver pantry, where there was a modest collection of neglected and tarnished plate still remaining. Dr Caldwell indeed seemed surprised to see so much, and I said, "True enough, sir, in London it wouldn't have lasted a day in an empty house, but I fancy we've the peculiar righteousness of the parson in this again. We can be sure he's forbidden the villagers to lay a finger on anything here, and you'll notice that it all carries the Pangersbourne crest. The gipsies likewise wouldn't touch it on that account, as crested property is always difficult and dangerous to dispose of. And this," I added, reaching into the darkest corner of one of the shelves, "may be what we're looking for."

It was a pretty little Queen Anne grinder, which rattled with whatever was still inside when I shook it. "We shall soon see," I said, unscrewing the top and tipping out the contents into the palm of my hand. A quantity of dust, and black peppercorns right enough; but also about half the amount of a different kind of smoother, shinier seed. "Well?" I demanded.

The doctor examined the mess narrowly, and

nodded. "There's no doubt of it. That's laburnum. It's most damnably cunning. The stuff would grind out with the pepper, and the strong flavour of that would cover any other taste."

"How much?" I asked. "And how long would it take?"

"Come now, sir," he protested, "I doubt even a physician could answer that. But so far as I'm informed the active principle's deadly. If the man was addicted to highly spiced foods he'd consume more than enough, and I guess it wouldn't take all that long."

"It's a devilish, diabolical business," I burst out. "I'm pretty sure of all of it now, yet the only evidence we've got is this stuff and gossip. We don't even know the precise course of events. Only Amelia Lydia can tell us that, and I'll be damned if I'll be responsible for asking her. In short without implicating the child I don't see how we're ever to bring this wicked rascal to book."

"Then you're convinced she introduced the laburnum seed to the peppermill?"

"I'm never convinced of anything until I have it all before me," I replied testily. "But I don't believe there's any other way it could have been done. Neither Smallbrook nor the woman Gossive would have dared to be seen about the kitchens or the silver pantry here after their quarrel with Pangersbourne, and what they had in mind. And I can think of a dozen tales they might have told a gullible and lonely child to induce her to put the stuff in this thing." I stopped short on that, struck by yet another of my sudden rays of illumination, and then added, "And begod Mrs Oakes at the inn can very likely tell us what it was. She knows something. That's why she warns us to have a care of the girl's safety."

But before Dr Caldwell could say anything to this

there was a sudden uproar outside. Maggsy's dulcet tones and his feet clattering on the floor tiles, Jagger complaining, "I don't like to hit a parson on the nose," and the Reverend Hangbolt's pulpit voice roaring, "Let me pass, you rascals; how dare you impede me?" as he came stomping into the kitchen in a rare beef-faced fury. "By God, sir," he declared, "here's a damned impudence. By what right d'you have those keys and enter this house?"

"The right of the law, sir," I replied simply.

"The law fiddlesticks," he retorted. "Whatever you may be in London, you've no authority here."

"Come, sir," I said, "if you want to discuss this rough I've no objection, but I'd as soon have it civil. I've the authority as representing the interests of Amelia Lydia Clarissa Pangersbourne, being duly appointed thereto by Lady Dorothea Hookham-Dashwood and Mr Dashwood, Member of Parliament." I thought I heard Doctor Caldwell behind me give a smothered snort, which he covered with a cough, and I asked the parson suddenly, "Do you know what this is?"

I showed him the peppermill; and somewhat nonplussed he gazed first at me and then at that and back again. "A pepper-grinder. What fresh damned nonsense is this?"

His very surprise proved his innocence, and I said, "Precisely," satisfied that at least the reverend gentleman knew nothing about the laburnum devilment. "I merely wish to ascertain whether all of the Pangersbourne silver is still here; again touching the interests of Amelia Lydia."

"So far as I can say," he answered. "I don't pretend to have an inventory; but it should be."

"Under your care and protection," I said. "And very proper. So we're doing famously. Now we've already

127

touched on the unfortunate death of Thomas Grubbage, and whether that might have to be taken further or not ain't quite certain yet. There's another matter first. The late Lord Pangersbourne conducted his own business affairs, did he not? That is, he did not employ lawyers or land agents."

The parson knew what was coming plain enough now, but he put a brave face on it. "It was a whim of his. He didn't trust 'em. There was a disagreement of some sort some years back."

"Seemingly he didn't trust banks or investments either. Which is understandable considering the losses incurred by the family further back still. Or he might have been evading this iniquitous damned Income Tax; and who can blame him, at a shilling in the pound. That's no affair of mine, and I don't mean it to be. But what I'm coming to, Mr Hangbolt, is that since his lordship's death there's been nobody to collect his rents or other dues. In short, every cottager or farmer on this estate has been living rent-free for the last twelve months. And hoping that happy state of affairs may long continue."

"Neither is that any business of mine," he announced. "Is that all, sir?"

"Not quite," I said. "I observe again that you're protecting your parishioners, and repeat that it's a credit to you. But it's a state of affairs which can't last for ever. My good friend Lady Dorothea is bound to request me to nominate trustees to administer the property on behalf of Amelia Lydia, and it might not be beyond my good nature to put up the sort who'll give a nod, wink, and blind eye to what's done with. I never see any good in raking up the past unless I'm forced to. On the other hand if there's any other claimant, or if the child or ourselves happen to suffer any other irritations, we could easily get saddled with the sort of damned pettifogging fellows who'll never stop asking questions and scrutinising every last farthing that might be due. D'you take my meaning?"

Once again I heard the strangely muffled sound from Dr Caldwell, but the parson started, "I take it that like all Bow Street Runners you're a damned . . ." but then checked himself, breathing hard. "Very well," he got out. "What d'you propose?"

"An open discussion. Questions answered freely on both sides," And let him have time to reflect on it, I thought. "But not here and now, sir, for we've other occasions pressing, and any minute I shall have my men complaining about keeping their breakfast waiting. Shall we say at the rectory later in the day? At a suitable hour to crack a bottle of Madeira with me and Dr Caldwell here?"

"If that is your wish," he snapped, and turned away, but I called, "Stay a minute, sir; have you heard any word of your Blacksmith Ironband yet?"

"We have not," he replied.

"That's unfortunate for your cricket match," I observed. "But did you not send the apprentice out to inquire?"

"The apprentice? That fellow wouldn't have the wit even to find himself if he were lost. All he discovered was that Ironband drank a quart of ale in The Cricketer's Tavern, out of Ringwood on the road back here."

"Well sir," I said, "you've been open with us, and I hope we understand each other better now. It's no fault of mine if we don't, and my offer still holds good. If you can find my coachman a horse he'll go to look for your man."

Jagger turned on his horse grin, but the reverend

129

gentleman gazed at him and me thoughtfully for a minute and then seemed to give a kind of shudder. "I thank you, sir, but no. We'll make our own further inquiries."

With that he took himself off as if he wasn't just sure of what he might add if he stayed longer; no more was said about the house keys, and Dr Caldwell murmured softly, "Mr Sturrock, I hope to God you may never turn your attention to politics."

As I explained, it was one of those offers a gentleman makes only so long as he knows it won't be taken up, but we now knew where Ironband had been last seen, and there was no reason why Jagger should not still begin there after he had driven me and the doctor to Wittings End; it would be an agreeable excursion for the good fellow. So first depositing the keys of the house safely in my valise we set off sharp after breakfast, leaving any further questions to Mrs Oakes for a later occasion as she was not in the best of tempers again, and putting Maggsy in charge of the calamity child with strict instructions not to let her out of his sight.

The doctor was somewhat dubious about this, and I was not all that easy myself, but it was the best we could do. Four in a chaise as well as the driver makes an uncomfortable party, not least for the horses, and I did not want her listening to our discussion with Dr Birdlip, as I also wanted Jagger free to go about his own business. Moreover, left to herself with Maggsy for most of the day she might well chatter out a bit more yet without being asked anything in particular, and we still needed the certain information that would put a rope round Master Smallbrook's neck. "It's a risk," I agreed as Jagger touched his cattle and we moved off. "But let me get that and I'll build a case to keep the child out of

130

it. And Maggsy's a good watch-dog and has a fondness for her. I'd be sorry for any rascal who tried mischief if he's within kicking distance."

The hour was still conveniently early, the day fine but with a brassiness in the air which very likely threatened more rain later on. The geese honking on the green, and women and children at their cottages, one man rolling the grass in preparation for the cricket match tomorrow, the parson riding out on a fat cob and looking as sultry as the weather. The two ancients, Aaron and Moses, sitting side by side angling solemnly in that sinister mill pool, and watching us like a pair of horrid gargoyles as we rattled past; the gipsies about their own mysterious business with a string of ponies in their encampment, but not without lookouts posted by the road for I noted several pairs of inquisitive eyes in the bushes on either side. "They'll all know we're out of the way," Dr Caldwell observed.

"So they will," I said. "And before long several people will be asking each other what we're about."

For the rest, however, the journey was uneventful with Jagger keeping up a steady clip, but for once in his life driving like a gentleman—no doubt bent on impressing the doctor—instead of pitching us about like peas in a colander. In short it was an interlude for reflection and genteel conversation; though how far it was likely to remain genteel when we came up with Dr Birdlip might be another matter.

Being a more bustling place than Milton Pangersbourne—as it could not very well be less—Wittings End boasted several taverns and a coach inn with conveyances to hire, and we paused here to make our further arrangements and give Jagger his instructions. These, in brief, to set out all along the way to The Cricketers at Ringwood and inquire after the missing blacksmith anywhere on the road where he might have been noted. "And we'll make this place our rendezvous," I finished. "But if we've done with Dr Birdlip before you return we shall hire a chaise to take us back to Pangersbourne and you can follow after. So now you may first put us down in Badger's Lane at Garden House."

This proved to be a moderately commodious establishment in red brick, built about the time of the second George, having circular steps to the front door and facing straight on the road behind posts and chains, with a side entrance, coach-house, outbuildings and pretty extensive grounds behind. A doctor in a fair way of practice or private means by all the appearances; and damnation important with it, for no sooner had we pulled on the bell than the door was flung open and a fattish, reddish, flusterish woman in a bib and apron bobbed out crying, "Round the side for attention."

"Doctor Birdlip," I said, but she went on in a kind of litany, "Leeches or tooth-pulling, physic or boils or lancing, down the side for Pickering."

"Doctor Birdlip," I repeated, "the coroner," and she repeated, "It's all the same, down the side, report it to Pickering."

"Be damned to Pickering," I announced. "Doctor Birdlip I say. It's about an uncommon vegetable."

"Pesty things," she observed, "the place is full of 'em," and shut the door in our faces.

By this time Dr Caldwell was showing further signs of quiet amusement at the curiosities of English rural life, though I was breathing somewhat heavy down my nose. But there was nothing for it except to do as the creature advised, and like a damned tradesman I led the way round to a yard by the coach-house, where there was another door which flew open to reveal a further oddity. A cadaverous young fellow in his twenties, as lanky as a bean-pole in rusty clothes, with a lock of hair falling down over his eyes, a look of being fresh from the anatomising rooms at St Bart's, and a most fearful eagerness about him. "Attention is it, gentlemen?" he cried. "Step this way please. We've all the latest remedies."

"Doctor Birdlip," said I yet again, but this one shook his head earnestly. "I wouldn't, gentlemen. Not if I was you. He was at it again last night. Shaky of the hand, if you take my meaning; and testy in his manner. If it's a nice bleeding you're after, I'm your man. You have the look of a rather full habit, sir."

"Be damned to your bleeding," I rapped at him, and might have added a fair bit more, had not Dr Caldwell caught my eye. I likewise caught his point that we might have a useful witness here, and modified my tone a little. "You're Dr Birdlip's understrapper, are you? And how long have you been with him?"

The fellow seemed puzzled, but answered willingly enough. "Near two years, God help me. For my sins. Though I dunno what I've done to deserve it. You wouldn't think that a rollick with a wench or two'd land you with this. Valuable experience for a young beginning physician in a genteel practice to the landed gentry. My oath it is."

"Precisely," said I. "And it's the landed gentry we want to talk about."

"Is it now?" He cast an uneasy glance across the yard, to an open gateway through which we could see the corner of a garden. "Then you'd best step inside. He's out there somewhere, and descends when you least expect him like the doom of God."

"You make him sound like some kind of monster," I observed, now much amused myself as we followed Mr Pickering into a sort of emporium liberally equipped

133

with bottles, jars, specifics and various horrid implements. "And you don't seem to care for him all that much."

He shook his head once more. "I love him like my father. And he ain't a monster, y'know. Or not quite. You might say he's a walking barrel of port and piss. Or a bladder of bile on two legs. Or a red-faced, blue-arsed pomposity when he's in a good temper. Or several other things if you lie awake at night making 'em up like I do. But a fine old English gentleman otherwise." He paused in this rhetoric. "Anyway, who are you? And what d'you want?"

"A few simple answers to short questions," I said. "I'm Mr Jeremy Sturrock of Bow Street, London. And this gentleman is Dr Wilford Caldwell of the American Philosophical Society."

"American Philosophical Society? About some of his fanciful plants, is it?" He looked from me to Dr Caldwell and back again. "And Bow Street? That's the Runners, ain't it? We ain't killed anybody yet. Not so far as I know. Or leastways not deliberate."

"We're concerned with Dr Birdlip as Borough Coroner. How does he conduct his inquests?" I asked.

"Why, short and sweet. Views the cadaver. Decides what killed it. Tells the jury. Asks 'Does anybody disagree', and says 'So that's your verdict'."

"And is that never questioned?" Dr Caldwell inquired.

"You don't question Dr Augustus Aloysius Birdlip. It ain't worth the trouble." He looked from the doctor to me again with his mouth hanging open. "God's sake, you ain't trying to get the old so-and-so into the dogcart, are you? Glory be if you are. You get him into Newgate and I'll come to London if I have to walk there, just to poke an empty port-bottle through the bars at him."

"Come, young man, let's have less frivolity," I told him sternly. "It's unseemly. Content yourself with answering our questions. We're coming now to the late Lord Pangersbourne. He was a botanist and horticulturist, as it appears Dr Birdlip is also. What was the relationship between the two of 'em?"

"Like a couple of damned silly children. Each forever wanting something the other'd got."

Dr Caldwell gave his snort of a chuckle, murmuring, "That's not uncommon," but I continued, "Now cast your mind back to his late lordship's death. It was on a Sunday; July eight last, to be precise. Do you recollect anything of that occasion? There was a message brought here."

"That's right. Fellow was the parson's stable-man. We was just about to come to our dinner. The old such-and-such expects me to eat with him. Likes to have somebody to rollock at, and considers it below the dignity of the profession for a physician to sit with the servants; even one as low as I am."

"For God's sake get on with it," I cried The fellow was as bad as Maggsy.

He glanced at the door nervously. "Keep your voice down, will you? We don't want thunder and lightning. Fellow says 'Lordship's been took with a seizure'. Birdlip asked 'Is he dead?' Fellow says 'Couldn't nohow be deader'. Birdlip says, 'Then there's nothing I can do for him. Put him in a cool place and he'll keep till tomorrow. I'm just sitting to my dinner, and I never travel after that'."

I cast Dr Caldwell a significant look and turned back to Pickering. "And what was his manner after this unfortunate event?"

"Damnation thoughtful," said Pickering.

135

"So he went to Milton Pangersbourne on the Monday. And what did he say his lordship died of?"

"Acute inflammation of the intestine. Brought on by over indulgence in spices and ill temper. Pangersbourne often had bellyache which made him irritable." He gazed at me with his jaw dropping and a light of unholy hope in his eye. "God's teeth, you ain't proposing he poisoned the crackpot?"

"I'm not proposing anything," I said, "and that's a most improper suggestion."

I considered for a minute, reflecting that we were not learning a lot we didn't already perceive or surmise, though my never failing instinct told me there was more yet if we knew how to get at it. But for all his jesting manner Pickering was patently uneasy, and you didn't have to look far to see why if he was caught telling tales. He might be little better than a slave here but this place was his living; for unless he's got private means a young physician fresh out of the schools has to find a patron if he don't want to starve. In short, he'd talk easier in different surroundings, and he was the sort to enjoy a whiff of conspiracy.

"It sounds as if you might make life a bit easier for yourself, Mr Pickering," I observed. "But whether you do or not is your own affair. We're going to have a word or two with Dr Birdlip now, and when we've done with him we shall return to The Coach and Horses. Soon after that you'll receive a message to the effect there's a traveller been took sudden and seriously sick there. D'you follow me?"

There was a gleam of mischief in his eye also like that often seen in the little villain Maggsy. "I follow you," said he.

Dr Birdlip proved to be all that Pickering had

136

described, and a good bit more in several respects, but his garden was at neat as an old maid. Very much as Lord Pangersbourne's must have been at one time, I judged; not quite as big, though with a more extensive plant house set against the wall at the far end. All the beds set out square and precise, not a speck of weed to be seen in the gravel paths between 'em, some with the plants as spruce as soldiers, and others with specimens of a different sort growing between rocks and stones. Dr Caldwell was profoundly impressed, gazing about with a professional eye, murmuring, "Whatever else the man may be he's an uncommon fine horticulturist," and moving on to one of these aforesaid stone beds where he stopped short suddenly and called softly to me.

He was peering down at a cluster of smallish vegetables between the rocks, meaning nothing to me for they was no more than little rosettes of leaves, but he murmured, "Lewisias, Mr Sturrock. I'd say exceedingly uncommon still in this country; not discovered in America until ten years ago. And I'd be ready to swear that the last time I saw those plants they were in Pangersbourne's garden."

It did not signify much, except maybe that Birdlip was light-fingered, but before I could make any further observation we were saluted by a bellow like that of an enraged bull, and we turned to behold the amiable physician himself emerging from the plant house and advancing on us; a truly fearful sight. Of a purplish countenance which spoke of more than indulgence the night before, a yellowish eyeball eloquent of hell's own liver the morning after, he was brandishing an implement and bawling, "Mind where you put yer blasted feet. Who the devil are ye, and what d'ye want?"

"Come sir," I protested. "I'd have thought the pursuit of horticulture was a somewhat more peaceful occupation."

"Impident with it as well, are ye?" he demanded, peering down at those poor innocent vegetables—which even themselves seemed to be cowering from him—and then glaring back at me and Dr Caldwell. "What're ye nosing and poking about them things for?"

"Interesting, sir," Dr Caldwell interposed. "Unless I'm much mistaken *Lewisia brachycalyx* and *angustifolia*. Discovered on the Lewis and Clark expedition to Western America, and singular rarities. Indeed the only other person I've known to be cultivating them over here was the late Lord Pangersbourne."

That was a straight shot, and it stopped the man in the midst of another mouthful. He stood regarding us for an instant plainly uneasy, head down and yellow eyeballs damned near popping, and I tried another one myself. I said, "We're here on more business than botany, sir. We represent the heirs and assignees of his late lordship."

He seemed to turn a shade richer purple. "You represent what?"

"You heard me clear," I answered. "And I'll inform you further that we're also investigating the circumstances of the death of that gentleman."

"Then ye're a pair of fools," he retorted and farted rudely. "He's been in his grave these twelve months past, so what in damnation's left of him to investigate?" Barrel of port and piss as Pickering had described this obnoxious bladder, he was still shrewd enough. He knew we could never prove anything now by fair means. "What's more ye're a pair of bloody impostors," he added. "For I've the best of reasons for knowing that you can't be representing the heirs and assignees. So take yerselves off before I call my man to put you out."

For a minute even I was bereft of speech. Dr Caldwell

138

was of little help for he was gazing back at the windows of the house with a look of considerable surprise on his face, and before I could find a word that might be used with decency there was an interruption in the shape of a skimpy little maid who came cantering out, crying, "Dr Birdlip, sir!" She stopped with a rasp of gravel and a squeal just as I started, "By God, sir," cried again, "Dr Birdlip, sir, the gentleman you said to fetch you for is here," and bolted back again as fast as her legs could carry her, while Birdlip repeated, "Take yerselves off, I say," and bellowed, "Turnbull!"

On this another fellow started to advance from the plant house, and I observed, "We shall have a very tidy altercation here before long." Dr Caldwell however was now regarding this other man with interest, and he turned a singularly mild and deceptive look on our empurpled physician. "We'll certainly not intrude, sir," he said. "But before we leave pray allow me as a botanist to felicitate you on your skill and your garden." This seemed to mollify the fat Mohock a trifle, for he paused in the act of a further blast, even starting to look very near human; until the doctor next asked, "Tell me if you will, sir, do you have any correspondence with my very good friend James Hunter of Philadelphia?"

And begod that touched off a fresh explosion. I thought the barrel of wind would have a fit, for it was clear the question had struck him hard somewhere. He gobbled at us like a cock turkey for a minute and then let out a fresh bellow. "Turnbull," he roared, "fetch a pail of water. Fetch a muck-fork. Have these rascals out of here."

"Pray don't discommode yourself, sir," I told him. "We don't propose to remain. We don't find your company all that diverting."

Nevertheless it took a pot of claret back in The Coach and Horses to restore my own benevolent humour, after we had despatched one of the stable-lads to fetch Pickering as arranged. Neither was my temper all that much improved by Dr Caldwell's showing signs of his sometimes unseasonable amusement again, but when I observed that so far the excursion had proved to be a damned sleeveless errand he replied, "Well, no sir; I wouldn't say that precisely. I'd say there were certain things we might add up."

I looked at him sharply, and he continued, "One you couldn't know and the other you couldn't see as you had your back to it. But the man Turnbull our remarkable physician set to hollering for was Pangersbourne's second gardener when I was here last year. And the gentleman who'd arrived when the maid came out to fetch Dr Birdlip was your Captain Haggard; and the young lady from Virginia with him. They were standing looking out of the window for a minute; and seemingly almighty surprised to see you there." He paused to take a draught of his claret. "And the question did Birdlip have any correspondence with James Hunter of Philadelphia was a shot at random, but I guess the answer came pretty clear. It's all of a silver dollar to a dime that that explains the presence of the young lady."

"So ho," I said, just as quick on the uptake as he. "So you're proposing that Birdlip wrote to James Hunter to inform him of Pangersbourne's death."

He nodded. "Precisely. And requested Hunter to seek out the Virginian branch of the family and pass the information on." He paused again. "And Birdlip don't exactly seem a man who'd do that out of kindness."

"Indeed he's not. He'd mean to get something out of it himself." I pondered that for a minute. "Very well then, let's say that accounts for the young woman. But

140

it still leaves Captain Haggard."

"Aye," he agreed. "It still leaves Captain Haggard."

He seemed confounded mysterious of a sudden, but further discussion was cut short then by the appearance of Master Pickering, coming in all of a bustle with his black bag and seeming to fancy that the whole affair was a splendid jape arranged just for his benefit. "Well now," he cried, bestowing a fantastic wink on us, "which of you gentlemen requires my attention? What the devil did you say to the old windy-guts?" he demanded; and then asked, "Is that claret you're drinking?"

"It claims to be," I said, rapping on the table for the wench to bring a pot for him. "But restrain your boisterous manner, for we're about serious business now. We've a few questions for you, and we want straight answers. Let us have 'em and we might provide you with something that'll put a bridle on Dr Birdlip for the rest of his life. Or lead us wrong anywhere and you might be in trouble yourself. So first: were you aware that he had a wager of five hundred guineas with Lord Pangersbourne concerning an outlandish vegetable his lordship was cultivating?

My warning seemed to have had its effect, for Pickering answered promptly, "I was. Though I never believed it was for that much. I thought the old bladder was boasting. He gets talkative after his third bottle at night; before he falls under the table."

"And could he have met the wager if he'd lost?"

The fellow gave us another expansive wink. "I doubt it. He ain't nearly so well britched as he makes out."

"So it would be to his interest to nobble this plant. Which we know he did. But we'll come to that in a minute. You tell us he was informed of Lord Pangersbourne's death on the Sunday, and went to Milton

141

Pangersbourne on Monday. What was his manner at that time?"

"Devilish. And got worse. By Sunday night he was cursing his guts out that Pangersbourne was a cantankerous rogue to have died so sudden."

"From which we may take it that he had not collected the wager. For we know that the plant itself had succumbed some days before. Did he say much about that?"

"My oath he did. Plenty. Swore he'd have the money out of the estate one way or another."

"One way or another." I looked at Dr Caldwell, who nodded gently. "But we'll come back to that too. First, did he ever have any dealings with one Jonas Smallbrook?"

"Smallbrook?" Pickering repeated. "Why, he's often about. Bringing game and suchlike. He's a poacher."

"He's a good bit more than that," I observed. "In short, your Dr Birdlip instructed Smallbrook to dispose of the vegetable in question by placing lime or common household soda in the water-butt at the Pangersbourne plant house."

"Most likely common soda," Dr Caldwell interposed. "As that would not be so easily noticed."

Pickering stared at us both and then burst into a guffaw. "You mean to say the old pisspot didn't poison Pangersbourne himself, but he did poison his blasted plant. By God, that's rich."

"And that's enough," I rapped out at him. "We've told you, this is a serious matter. The destruction of that plant led directly to Pangersbourne's own death. Now then; did Dr Birdlip procure the keys of Pangersbourne House from Parson Hangbolt shortly after that event?"

142

For the first time our young man betrayed uneasiness, and I answered for him. "He told Hangbolt that he had heard certain rumours concerning the drowning of Thomas Grubbage, and he might reopen the inquest if he was pushed to it. Whereupon the parson loaned him the keys. So who searched the house? Birdlip, or you; or both?"

"See now," Pickering started, and then confessed, "Both of us. He don't have all that much bowels when it comes to anything, and I have to do what I'm told. Such as it might be the old bastard's my bread and butter, and he was determined to have his five hundred. He promised me an increase of wages if we found it."

"If you found the strong-box? But you didn't?"

He shook his head and even Dr Caldwell seemed surprised; a sufficiently unusual event. "A strong-box?" he asked.'

"In which several generations of Pangersbournes have kept their liquid assets since the South Sea Bubble," I explained. "Probably a very considerable fortune by now." I turned back to Pickering. "You did not find the strong-box. But you did find certain ancient title deeds referring to an estate in Virginia. Which Dr Birdlip removed; and thereafter he wrote a letter to America. And you put me in the way of that final illumination, sir, little more than an hour ago," I added handsomely to the doctor.

"You've a quick mind, Mr Sturrock," he observed.

"So so, sir," I said modestly. "So so. But there we have it, I fancy. And there you have it as well," I added to Mr Pickering, surveying him benevolently; which seemed to frighten his daylights out. There was no point in going too deep into the death of Thomas Grubbage, for there was little could be done about that now, but I continued, "Your Dr Birdlip was guilty of a gross dereliction of his duties as coroner by not inquiring deeper into the evidence at a certain inquest shortly after his lordship's death. As he was just as guilty of gross negligence as a physician by failing to perceive that his lordship had been poisoned by a malicious administration of laburnum seeds. "There's no need for you to know any more," I finished kindly. "But if that ain't enough for you to hold him on a tight rein in future you're never likely to make a smart physician yourself."

EIGHT

"It's by no means an uncommon practice," I told Dr
Caldwell as we returned to Milton Pangersbourne,
driving in a damned bone-shaking old rattler since
Jagger had not yet returned from his inquiries with our
own chaise. "After twenty years of war, to say nothing
of this damned Income Tax and various financial uncer-
tainties, nobody knows how many people choose to
keep their money in solid coin rather than depositing it.
And after their losses in the South Sea Bubble, then the
failure of so many of the county banks, you can understand the Pangersbournes getting even more eccentric
than most on the matter. A habit like that stays a long
time with a family."

"Nevertheless it was a smart piece of deduction," the
doctor was kind enough to observe.

"I have a nice instinct in such matters, sir," I confessed. "The absence of estate accounts or agencies, the
South Sea Company share certificates; the fact that his
lordship made his subscription to you in coinage of
various sorts, and only kept the smallest possible credit
to pay others by banker's order; the searching of the
house, all combined to set me thinking. I've no doubt
that when we come to inquire further we shall hear of a

145

lawyer somewhere; though seemingly there was a quarrel or disagreement in that area, very likely some years back, and thereafter my lord chose to manage his affairs himself. But what's more important is to find that strong-box and discover what's in it. I've a notion that together with the estate Miss Amelia Lydia could well prove to be a very wealthy child; yet we might have the devil's own job securing it all to her."

"Meaning Captain the Honourable Wilberforce Haggard and the young woman from Virginia?" Dr Caldwell asked.

"Meaning Captain the Honourable Wilberforce Haggard," I said.

But when we reached the inn all consideration of Captain the Honourable had to wait, for there were more direful happenings. Jagger had still not yet returned, Maggsy and the child were also absent, and Mrs Oakes was fretting to dish up her dinner. "Serve it," I said for the sake of the woman's temper, and the doctor and I sat to the table alone, though prey to the liveliest misgivings, and did less than justice to an excellently well crackled young loin of pork with apple sauce, etc., while I questioned the woman closely as she bustled in and out. She could not keep her eyes on the child for ever, she declared, and that horrible boy of mine was quite wicked enough to look after her; neither had there been any stone-throwing or fighting again with the village children or anybody else, as Parson Hangbolt had given strict orders that we were all to be left well alone.

Pressed further she added that for some time after the doctor and myself had left with Jagger that morning they had sat on the bench outside the inn, plainly wondering what to do with themselves. She herself had been mopping out the tap after the dirty pigs of men last night, having the window open to blow out the beastly stink of 'em, and for what little she cared she had noted that the child was in a cantankerous humour, twitting Maggsy that she knew of something she could show him if she had a mind to. "So ho," I said. "And what was that?"

"God's sake," the woman cried, "don't ye think I'd got something better to do than listen to 'em? Oakes've took herself off to Lyndh'st to be out of your way, and I'm here on my own. I went up the stable loft to make the beds of your two rascals and empty their pots. But for what it may be worth the boy come thumping in while I was there, snatched a candle out of the stick and went galloping off again."

"A candle?" I repeated. "What did he want that for?"

"Didn't say, nor I didn't ask," she replied. "Nor I don't have time to stand here clapping with you. All you bliddy men're the same. Bone-idle yerselves, and fancy everybody else is as well."

"You take a somewhat jaundiced view of us," I observed. But neither did we have time to remain here bandying words, for I did not like the look of this situation, and I demanded, "Jonas Smallbrook? Have you seen him about?"

"I en't," she answered briefly. "Nor her wasn't in the tap last night. The rascal often goes off in the forest for days at a stretch. But that don't signify a lot, and I've got work to do." She stopped at the door gazing at us. "And so hev you to ef you ask me. You'd best go to look for that child."

We had no great need of that advice either but at least we now had a fair idea of where to start. If Maggsy had fetched a candle there could only be one place he would

147

want it for, though I hastened up to my room to make doubly sure; and, as I expected, the keys to Pangersbourne House were no longer where I had left them for safety, in the secret bottom of my valise. "I'll have his guts for this frolic," I promised, and then turned to charging and priming my pistols with particular care.

I left a last word with Mrs Oakes that Jagger was to follow us on the instant when he returned and we set off. "The reckless, chuckle-headed, blue-arsed ape," I said as we hurried on our way. "You'll recollect the child told Maggsy that a day or so before the fatality Lord Pangersbourne had her sent to her room with the housekeeper and kept there, as she'd observed him about some private business? There's only one thing that could have been. The little calamity knows where the strong-box is, and Master Maggsy's talked her into going to open it."

At first sight there was no appearance of mischief as we approached the house. It merely seemed desolate under a sky lowering for rain once more, no movement in any of the dark windows, and the front door still shut and locked. But in the stableyard there was first of all another door to the rear premises left open, and then a scrap of fanciful cambric lying near the garden archway. "And that," I announced as we took it up, "is one of the dozen handkerchiefs I had purchased for the calamity in Oxford Street; when we were fitting her out with her necessities a few weeks back."

The doctor made a great business of studying the position of the rag and its distance from the house, etc., before making his pronouncement. "And I'd guess she dropped it leaving here. So what does that tell us?"

"Why, sir," I said, "simply that she left here. But it don't say a lot about what might have happened in there." It was a bit short, and as I had no wish to offend the well-meaning gentleman I hastened to make amends. "But an acute observation none the less. So to save time will you take a further look about the garden, while I see what there is in there; if anything by now."

"A wise proposal," he agreed amiably, and went off like a beagle on the scent, while I turned in through the doorway, cocking my pistol and standing there an instant to listen.

All was as silent as the tomb, however, and nothing fresh to be seen in the disorder of the sculleries and kitchen, though when I went up the domestic stairs to the hall I thought for a minute that I heard a soft, strange bumping sound coming from somewhere. Whatever it might have been it ceased as I stood listening once more, the silence became profound again and I hastened up to the study; for that place, I thought, was the heart of the mystery in this damned house. But neither was there anything suspicious here.

By this time I was pretty certain that the scent was cold, for if Mrs Oakes was to be believed the mischievous wretches had left the village at mid-morning, and it was now wearing on into late afternoon. And if Master Maggsy was still in the house he must have heard me about, for my own footsteps were echoing like drum beats and the rascal had the ears of a cat. Yet there was no doubt that they had been here, and the candle could only mean that they meant to venture into a cellar or passage of some sort without windows, which must be somewhere about the lower floor.

In my wide and varied experience I have been in some singular establishments, the worst stews of London, the sewers of Wapping, the Haymarket gambling-dens and curious whore-shops, but never had I been in anything more gruesome than that seemingly respectable Queen

Anne country house on a lowering August afternoon. As my diligent readers will appreciate, I am not a fanciful man, but there were shadows everywhere; and no sooner had I returned to the hall that same strange knocking started again. A few beats, and a stop, and then a few more; and impossible to tell where it was coming from. "Be damned to this," I announced, and set to flinging back all the several doors there one after the other, making noise enough to waken the dead. Two or three ante-chambers, a dining-room and a once handsome withdrawing salon in the Adams style, all enshrouded in dust and cobwebs, and lastly a small library.

And here I stopped. I said, "Here we have it," for there was the still persistent stink of a sulphur match in the stagnant air. Finger marks on one of the tables, a spot of grease from a candle, and a mess of footprints in the dust, especially by one of the bookcases, though at first sight you couldn't make much of 'em except that some were small enough to be Amelia Lydia's. "So ho," I said, gazing at the book-shelves, and that one in particular; one of a pair set either side of a deep fireplace.

These were of the open sort, without glass fronts, built near enough up to the ceiling and well filled with books, though in this one some had been taken out and tossed down anyhow. "So that's what the child saw Lord Pangersbourne doing," I observed. But on that the doctor called from the hall, and entered looking a trifle grim, holding out a scrap of something for my attention and announcing simply, "You'll know what that is."

"I do," I said at once. It was a little bow, in narrow pink satin ribbon sewn in the shape of a lover's knot. "It's from the sprigged muslin dress she's so fond of.

There's one of these at each sleeve and another at the neck. Where did you find it?"

"By the garden gate to the park. I guess she's a very, very clever little girl. There's no sign of a struggle, for the gravel's still damp enough to show it if there had been. But she went with two others, one each side of her; and she's dropping these things to show us the way. What of the boy?" he asked.

"He's here somewhere. Not least as it would need more than two to take him and the girl. And there's a sound of muffled knocking from time to time. They started in this room and passed through that." I nodded at the book-case, and once you'd seen it the rest was easy, even to a catch inside the case, for when you released that the entire construction swung away from the wall on hinges and castors. Or it merely seemed easy, for there we were baulked. Behind the case there was another flush door set in the oak panelling; with no handle to it but only a keyhole. And try as we might that was locked and immovable.

"So . . ." said the doctor. "There we have it," said I. "And it's very plain that the rascals who carried the child off have now got the keys as well."

"Then we shall need axes for that," he observed.

"At the least," I agreed. "Moreover, it's very likely iron-plated on the other side. And if we go to procure axes and lanterns the entire village will know what we want them for in a matter of minutes."

He glanced at me somewhat curiously. "So which do we look to first? The girl or the boy?"

"It's a nice choice," I confessed. "I'd say neither."

"You'd say what?" The doctor rarely allowed himself to show surprise, but he now gazed at me in open astonishment. "Did I hear you correctly, sir? Are you aware of what you're proposing?"

151

"Quite correctly," I assured him. "And I am perfectly aware. We shall do best to let events take their own course for a while. And this is an excellent opportunity for our discussion with Parson Hangbolt."

The good gentleman seemed to fancy that I was a kind of monster, and by the time we found ourselves approaching the rectory I was growing a little impatient. "Sir," I announced at last, "I know of nobody better able to take care of himself than Master Maggsy. He was born in the stews and passed his first childhood as a chimney boy. And that means he's as resourceful as a fox, and can work his way out of pretty near anything."

"Maybe," said the doctor. "But I still hold that you're taking an almighty improper chance. And it still don't account for the girl."

"It don't," I agreed. "But if the people who caught 'em in the house had meant murder they'd have done it there and then. As it is Master Maggsy's entertaining himself by knocking and banging—and no doubt reflecting on his rashness—while Amelia Lydia's in the gipsies' encampment. Recollect that she's been there before and she knows 'em. Moreover, I see the hand of Captain Haggard in this, and I'm starting to get some curious notions about that gentleman. But whatever he may be if he's there we can say that the young woman from Virginia's also somewhere close by; and we can be yet more certain that she's not the sort who'll stand by and see a child come to any harm."

He still shook his head, however. "We can only hope to God you're right. But I don't like it, Mr Sturrock. Nor I don't see what you're getting at either."

"Making sure the child don't learn things about herself that she shouldn't ever know," I said. "And

152

where she is now nobody's likely to tell her. In short she's better off there for a bit."

By now we were at the rectory and the discussion was cut short. Parson Hangbolt must have observed us approaching through the churchyard, for he opened the door to us himself; though not overwhelming with welcome. Nevertheless he led us into a kind of study, which was more cluttered with cricketing gear than the respectable works you might expect a parson to have about him, bade us shortly to be seated and then asked, "Well, sir; you'll be brief I trust?"

"As brief as we can," I promised in my most benevolent manner. "And to that end I shall tell you simply that we came to Milton Pangersbourne with only one purpose. Namely, to determine the status of the child, Amelia Lydia. To be sure we've discovered a number of other little oddities as well," I added. "But we'll not fret ourselves with those; or not unless we're forced to. So let's start with Roderick Pangersbourne; who was killed at Corunna. It's a plain, simple question. Did he, or did he not, marry a woman named Clara Comfrey, who also called herself Clarissa du Frésne de Champillion, some time about 1802?"

For a minute it looked as if we were about to get a dusty answer before the reverend gentleman had second thoughts. "He went through a form of marriage," he said, and I pounced on that at once, for this was what I had most feared. "A form of marriage?"

"Must you have the whole unsavoury story?" he demanded, and I replied sternly, "We must, sir. I'll remind you once more that we've discovered several little oddities about this village. On the other hand nothing you tell us need go beyond the four walls of this room." And I had the best of reasons now for seing that it didn't.

153

He regarded me with evident distaste again, and then started, "Very well. You will understand first that although Roderick was wild and irresponsible I had a certain indulgence for him, as he was an excellent cricketer. He was just down from Rugby school, but showed no inclination for going on to Oxford."

"So ho," I observed. "So he had time for mischief. And being a cricketer he would be a close friend of your Blacksmith Ironband."

That shot seemed to discompose the parson still more, for his answer was too sharp. "Ironband has nothing to do with it," he said, and continued quickly, "I believe Roderick met this woman at a theatrical performance in Salisbury the year before. And he was plainly besotted. In the early summer of 1802 he asked me to marry them myself. I refused. I told him it was impossible under the terms of the Hardwicke Marriage Act of 1753. He was a minor, and Lord Pangersbourne would never give his consent since the woman was clearly an undesirable. She was undeniably attractive but everything about her was false, from the ridiculous name she passed under to the story that her parents were French aristocrats who had fled the Terror in Paris in '93."

"It's a living wonder," I marvelled. "They all tell the same tale. You'd be surprised how often I've heard it. But a marriage of some sort did take place? And there is a record in a Parish Register?"

"There is. I have seen it myself."

"Then how in damnation was it done?"

"Pray moderate your language in my house," he reproved me. "They presented a forged special licence. I have examined that too. I do not know how it was procured; but the signatures on it were good enough to deceive the clergyman, who was already elderly and of

154

failing sight. And I understand that Roderick made some excuse about going for the army and wishing to leave the woman secure. That much at least was true. Pangersbourne had purchased a minor commission for him several months before."

"To keep him out of trouble, no doubt. Where was this marriage?"

"In Lyndhurst. But unless I must I shall not disclose the name of the church or the incumbent. He is now a very old man, very elderly and almost totally blind. I will not have distress brought on him." The parson stopped, then finished heavily, "In my opinion you will do well to let this sorry business rest where it is."

"I only hope we may." I looked at Dr Caldwell and he took my meaning. If there were any other claimants to the estate, and this lot got out, Amelia Lydia might whistle for her share for ever. "What name did the woman sign?" I asked.

"What was presumably her real name. Clara Comfrey."

"And until that time Roderick had only known her as Clarissa du Frésne de Champillion?"

The Reverend nodded, seemingly not trusting himself to speak, and I continued to Dr Caldwell, "And there we have it. The woman was in a cleft stick. The marriage licence was good enough so long as nobody asked too many questions; but she was quick to see that if she gave her fancy name Roderick himself might declare the marriage invalid when he discovered the truth and the gilt began to wear off the gingerbread. He discovered too late that he had been made a fool of. A sorry story indeed, sir," I added to Mr Hangbolt, for whom I was now beginning to feel a certain respect. "And you may be assured that we shall use it with the utmost discretion. But might I ask how you have so

155

much information?"

"His Lordship requested me to make the investigation when the child was brought here at a few days old. As you may already know she was brought to the inn by one of these theatrical persons. There was a letter with her which said that she was Roderick's child, that Roderick had married Clara Comfrey and deserted her from the altar about a month before the birth; that she had died in childbed, the theatrical company was about to break up, and there was nobody to care for the baby. To do Pangersbourne justice, he accepted the charge; he was eccentric and frequently irascible, but not heartless. I recollect him saying that it was a case of the sins of the son descending on the father; but he also said that someone had to make amends to the child. I baptized her myself."

"And does this letter still exist?" I asked.

He shook his head. "I do not know. And I hope that is the last of your questions."

"There must be one or two more," I said. "But I promise that any you may still be good enough to answer will help to make those amends. And we've got it pretty clear by now." All except the most curious questions, I reflected, wondering how best to frame my next. "So Roderick left to join his regiment immediately after that unhappy marriage. And no more was heard of him until the news of his death at Corunna in 1809. How was his lordship apprised of this unfortunate event?"

"By Roderick's commanding officer, when the expeditionary force finally returned to England. To be exact he was first posted missing during the last stages of the retreat on Corunna from Sahugun. His death was confirmed later." Now plainly uneasy the parson stopped, and then added, "No doubt if I don't tell you

156

you'll continue to pry. His death was confirmed by Ironband."

"By Ironband?" I repeated. "Then he was at Corunna as well?"

"He was a sergeant in Roderick's company. Wounded and one of the few survivors of the rearguard. As you will know the army retreated for three hundred miles through the mountains; over sixteen days and in winter conditions." He got up and went to the door to open it for us. "Beyond that I have nothing more to say. Except to beg you again in the name of Christian charity to let all this be."

So far the doctor had remained silent, only watching and listening with his air of quiet thought. But here he murmured, "And I guess that's something again that the child should never know?"

"It is," the parson answered shortly. "And now if you'll give me leave I've other matters to attend to."

"Why, willingly," I announced as we rose ourselves. "Yet there is one more question you might answer without harm to anybody, and I'll put it short. Was the village in general aware that Lord Pangersbourne kept the greater part of his portable wealth in a strong-box?"

He gave us a brief and bleak smile. "Servants see everything; and servants chatter."

"As we're all too well aware," I agreed. "But where did he keep the box itself? Commonly a gentleman would have a thing like that under his own eye, in his study. But it's not there now. Which leads me to ask did his lordship have any building alterations made in Pangersbourne House at some period? Most likely about 1804?"

Doctor Caldwell looked at me inquiringly, and I went on to explain to him. "We were living in daily expectation of an invasion from France by Bonaparte at that

157

time, and this place is not all that far from the coast. A great many people in the like situation had shelters built and hiding-places constructed for their valuables."

The parson nodded. "That is so." He seemed relieved to have something he could answer freely. "I presume you wish to find this box to the benefit of the child? Very well. It was in the study. I saw it there myself on several occasions. But Pangersbourne was particularly concerned with the rumours of invasion, although he swore that not all the Frenchmen in the world would cause him to leave here. Nevertheless he did have alterations made. He brought in workmen from Salisbury. There was an old wine-cellar, I understand. He had the original entrance below stairs built up, and opened another concealed in the library on the ground floor. As you observe, in 1804."

"So there we have that also," I said. "We're still more profoundly obliged to you, sir. We shall look to meeting you at your cricket match with all this unhappy business cleared up and safely behind us. And if your Mr Ironband has not returned by then you may play my man Jagger in his place."

And I little knew what a strange result that generous offer was to have.

"Well, sir," I announced as we passed through the churchyard, "several days since Master Maggsy observed that we might do little more than rake up the muck here, and we've raked it up with a vengeance. What we have to do next is to find a way to bury it decently again."

"I'd have guessed that what we have to do next is to find a way to get your unfortunate young man out of that cellar," he replied.

There was an unwonted asperity about him, and I

158

said, "Why, to be sure. But you'll note that we now know how to set about it without a deal of noise and fuss. I never yet heard of a wine-cellar without a ventilator of some sort to it."

"What?" he demanded, for the second time startled out of his amiable calm. "D'you mean to claim you had that in mind when we went to talk to the parson?"

"A mere thought," I answered with my own modesty. "It crossed my mind that a little inquiry might be easier and quieter than breaking doors down with axes." For a moment I suspected he was about to say he did not believe me, but I continued, "And we've learned much else of interest from the reverend gentleman. Not least that Lord Pangersbourne had his strongbox moved in 1804. But you will note that it was still there in 1802."

The doctor looked sideways at me. "Which brings us back again to Captain Wilberforce Haggard?"

He was quick in his thinking; as quick as I am, and I know nobody quicker. "Precisely," I said. But before I could add any more we were stopped short by an astonishing and perplexing vision reeling at us through the gravestones.

The ancient gravedigger in his smock, brandishing his scythe fearfully like Death itself; Jagger most excessively drunk; and Miss Amelia Lydia doing her small best to support the rascal. "Have'n out of here; it en't proper in my graveyard," screeched the gravedigger; "What ho, guv'nor; I found'n," bawled Jagger; "He's as boozed as a fiddler's bitch," observed Miss Amelia in her ladylike accents, "and what he needs is a pail of water over his head."

"He needs a horse-trough," I announced. "Jagger, you damned villain, what've you been doing?"

"Find'n the blacksmith," said Jagger. "That's what

you said, ain't it? Well, I found'n. An' if you think I'm pissed you wait 'til you see Ironband. So'd you be if you'd had a pot in every public between Ringwood an' here. Goramighty there's hundreds of'm; thoushands. Good day to you, sir," he added politely to Dr Caldwell, then sitting back heavily on to a tombstone and muttering. "Whoa there, the hoshes; steady me beauties, the roads is a bit bumpy tonight."

I shall not dwell on the unseemly spectacle. "Get'n off'f that," the horrid ancient screeched again, " 'tes blasphemy and worse, and I'll fetch the pa'son to 'ee." And that was more than enough. Between us we heaved the wretch to his feet and marched him out through the lychgate, with the ancient uttering maledictions behind us; and there Miss Amelia Lydia chose to explode her own little bombshell, for I demanded wrathfully, "And what have you done with the horses and my chaise, you damnable villain?"

"They're quite safe," said she. "The stable-boy at the inn is putting up the horses. The lady drove us back."

"The lady?" I demanded, so astonished that I let Jagger fall again. "For God's sake, child, what lady?" although it was plain enough that there could only be one.

"The lady at the gipsy camp," she explained kindly, as if I was addled in my wits as well. "I was there a long time, wondering why you didn't come although I left things for you to follow me by. But it didn't matter because I know most of the gipsies quite well, and they're much kinder than the people in Wapping, and they gave me some most delicious baked hedgehog for my dinner."

"Be damned," I cried, foreseeing a long and rambling tale, foreseeing also that we might have to work uncommon fast now if we were to save much, "let

160

explanations wait. I know most of 'em anyway. Let's get this reckless scoundrel sobered as quick as we can, and then go to find Maggsy."

The first was accomplished in the simplest manner possible by having the rascal under the pump at the horse-trough outside the inn. Within a very short space he was rueful, regretful and profane; but in his right mind. Then after that I gave my orders. Stable lamps, my pistols, crowbars, hammers, chisels and other implements; and as an afterthought Blacksmith Ironband's apprentice, for he was a brawny young fellow and might as well do the heavy work.

Needless to say these preparations were watched with lively curiosity by Mrs Oakes, Aaron and Moses, and several more of the idle villagers, and the last thing I wanted was to have one or another of them giving warning to anybody. But there was no time for niceties, and I told Mrs Oakes, "Keep 'em back; have the women keep their men indoors." Nevertheless old Aaron and Moses still inquired, "What be about of then?" and I am never short of a better thought. I announced, "We're going to have Thomas Grubbage out of his grave, and if you lot know what's good you'll stay where you are while we're at it."

That steadied 'em, and they remained in a huddle, watching us and muttering wickedly, but not following as we set off. Then it was time to question Amelia Lydia a bit more, and I said, "Let's have it quick and short now, miss. We know two men took you off. Who were they, and was they carrying anything else?"

"Abel Tickner and a gentleman," she replied promptly. "Abel Tickner had a kind of leather pouch out of the big box, and was grumbling that they might have brought more. The gentleman said it wouldn't be

161

wise in daylight as they might be seen, and they had to make arrangements about horses, but he took some papers. And I thought he looked . . ."

"That don't matter for now," I interposed, fearful lest she might let out too much. We'll have the rest of your tale when there's time for it. So we can be pretty sure they'll come back," I added to the doctor. "Most likely at just about darkening."

After that little more was said until we came round the house to the stableyard, by this time with the evening wearing on, though still an hour or so to dusk. Here I posted Jagger at the garden entrance to the park to keep watch, and then after that the rest was easy now we knew what to look for. This being a simple cast-iron grating set in the cobbles close under the building, and short work for our young bullock of a blacksmith and his implements; though the noise he made about it set all the rooks flapping up out of the elms behind us.

But the rooks was nothing to Master Maggsy as we clambered down through the aperture. There was a perfect storm of thumpings as we paused to put light to our lanterns, thus revealing a small brick chamber with no sign of a strong-box in it, but only another closed and locked door. "We've further to go yet," I observed. "At it my lad," and the good fellow needed no further encouragement, attacking the oak with such gusto that this too fell open in another minute.

Next lay a short passage, a flight of stone steps going upwards through a narrow aperture, and two more doors; one of these also locked, but the other merely barred on this side, and that bouncing and banging like a drum from Master Maggsy hammering at it within. He roared out like a Drury Lane demon when our blacksmith struck the bar off, uttering such observations as even I had never heard from him before, and

162

bawling, "They got Peggoty!" to which she screeched, "No they ain't, Maggsy dear," while he stopped short, blinking in the lamplight and then snarling, "Took you long enough to get here."

"Be quiet, both of you," I ordered, surveying the last door. That would do very well as it was, I decided, for it would hold them up for a minute to unlock it and that would be long enough for my purpose. But I could not have either the blacksmith or the child witnessing the final scene—especially the child—and I continued, "Take Amelia Lydia back to the inn; and no argument about it. We don't have time. You may go with them to get yourself a pot of ale to my account," I told our young Hercules. "And if you keep your mouth shut about this you might do better still yet."

Out in the yard again the light was now starting to fade and I hastened them on their way, then called Jagger back to show him what he had to do and made our final dispositions; these being very simple. Dr Caldwell was to have one of my pistols, post himself inside where he could watch for our men coming through the hall, and cover them from the rear when they opened the door in the library and began to descend the steps. I would put out the lantern and wait for them in the dark of the cellar. Jagger was to return to his station in the garden to sight them coming through the park and then bring me warning of their approach.

"We can't be sure of it," I said again. "With the child returned to us they might have taken fright. But I fancy there's a lot left in that strong-box yet. And my greatest hope is that Jonas Smallbrook will come with them to get a share."

And a damned sight more lasting share than he'd expect. To be short about it I meant to shoot the villain myself, for I still could not see any other way of bringing

163

him to book without getting Amelia Lydia into it. There would be a little accident in the confusion; and even that would be an end too kind and easy for a man who could use a child to convey poison. But, as you shall see, Providence had other and stranger plans for him.

As it happened we did not have long to wait. The square of the broken grating had barely faded before Jagger came back. He made very near as much noise as an elephant scrambling through, and I muttered, "Quiet, you scoundrel. How many? Smallbrook?"

"Three; and they've brought horses. Tethered at the garden gate," he answered. "But dunno otherwise, it's near enough dark. Might be though. One of 'em's smallish."

"Please God it is," I said, cocking my pistol and taking a position where I could get a good sight at the steps. Then again there was silence until we heard the scrape of boots in the yard; the creak of a door, and a little clatter from the kitchen; silence once more as they moved up to the hall; and at last the rumble of the bookcase as they pulled it back.

Jagger was blowing like a grampus, and I growled at him to hold his damned breath. A flicker of light now, and shadows down the steps; the canting voice of the gipsy, and Captain Haggard answering him; then Haggard appearing, bearing a lantern in one hand and the keys in the other; and Tickner, confound him, pausing on the bottom step and blocking my sight of whoever was behind him, crying, "See the doors there; they're open and the boy's gone."

"And so much the better, be damned to him," the captain replied. "We shall be gone ourselves in a minute." So that's the horses, I thought, and said to myself, "That's what you may think, sir," but Tickner

164

whined, "There's mischief here, I tell ye," and I cursed the rascal for he was standing in my line of fire, covering the figure behind, and I could not afford to waste my single bullet. Then however Haggard said, "God damn it, come and hold the lantern while I unlock this door," and he moved down the last two steps.

Now I had the other rascal in my sights, no more than a shape but good enough, for I am a deadly shot. My finger was on the trigger and in another breath I might have had a most vexatious death on my hands had not Dr Caldwell somehow guessed my intention. He called, "Hold there, Sturrock; it's the woman!"

In an instant all was confusion, though not for long, for they was trapped between the two of us and had little inclination to fight. Tickner tried to flatten himself against the bricks of the wall, but the woman cried, "God's blood, what is this? Sech impudence." And Captain Haggard said, "Put that pistol down, sir. We've a damned sight more right here than you have."

"Why, sir, no doubt about it," I agreed. "Lord Roderick Pangersbourne, is it not?"

NINE

Not yet aware of how much I knew or guessed about him my lord remained cool enough, and even gave a light laugh. "Why then, that's right; though I can't reckon how you know. Nor who the devil you are or what you're doing? I asked you that the other day but got no answer."

"You shall have it now, sir. Sturrock of the Bow Street Police. Investigating certain irregularities here."

"Irregularities?" he demanded. "There ain't any irregularities. A man may do as he pleases in his own house. So you may take yourself off."

I chose to let the rudeness pass. "We're not sure it is your house yet. That might hang on whether his late lordship died intestate or not. There's some doubt of the manner of his death, and I might have to inquire where you were at that time?"

"Me? God blast your impudence," he exploded. "I was in America. And Miss de Bourne here can bear me out. If it comes to that what was wrong with the old man's death? We were advised he died of an inflammation of the stomach."

"And so he did, sir. But the point at issue is who and what caused the inflammation. I might further find it necessary to question the man Ironband about events in the year 1809."

"Ironband?" That was very palpably a shot across his bows. By the involuntary look he shot at Miss de Bourne it was plain that there was something here he'd as soon she did not know; and not all that difficult to guess what it was. "What the devil's Ironband got to do with anything? For what use it may be to you Ironband's lying dead drunk at this minute. And has been these last three days."

"He'll sober up in time. But we can let all that pass for now, sir, for I must tell you that I'm also here to represent the proper interests of a child. And I fancy you should know who she is."

"Be damned to that," he started, but the woman interposed, "Mind what you say, Roderick," and looked unfavourably at Dr Caldwell and me. "And pray be good enough to uncock that pistol, sir," she added. "I know as much about those things as you do, and I don't fancy 'em like that."

I have noted American ladies' familiarity with firearms several times before, and somewhat amused I lowered the hammer, reflecting that our new Lord Pangersbourne had met his match here. But I continued, "Now sir, I propose that we all together examine what's left in your late father's strong-box."

"I'll see you in hell first," he retorted, but again Miss de Bourne put her firm foot down. "Open the dratted door, do, and be done with it," she cried. "This place gives me the grues. You can debate about it afterwards, if you must."

Dr Caldwell seemed as amused as I was, but the gipsy Tickner was clearly meditating escape now seeing the pistols disarmed. He was already edging past the doctor and there was still the matter of my watch. But I did not want any further distractions at present with more important business on hand, and he might even be more use to me elsewhere. I said, "Let him go, Jagger. We've got nothing against you or Jonas Smallbrook," I told the rascal in my kindest and most simple-faced manner. "You've both been very kind to little Amelia Lydia at one time or another, and if you're at the cricket tomorrow before we return to London I'll buy the pair of you as much ale as you care to drink. And maybe something more besides," I promised for the sake of telling the truth.

"To be sure, your honour," he babbled and grinned, plainly taking me for a fool. "To be sure and obliged, and we'll drink the little lady's health. And I'll go now to stand by the horses, Master Roderick, lovey dearie," he added, scuttling off up the steps like a rabbit, and thankful with it.

I could have told 'em that they were not likely to need horses tonight, but by now Pangersbourne had unlocked the door and we entered the cellar with our shadows flickering dark on the walls. This was a small white-washed chamber containing only a plain table and chair, and a wrought-iron chest set on a kind of raised stone settle; ancient, but oiled and well kept, and big enough to hold a king's ransom. "A curiosity in itself," I observed. "It must date back very near to the time of Queen Elizabeth."

"Sir," announced the forthright Miss de Bourne, "I don't care if it dates back to the time of Adam. Let's have it open."

But the lady's face showed a certain disappointment when Pangersbourne shot the two massive locks and finally lifted the heavy lid, for at first sight there was nothing much to make a fuss about. A few documents, several smaller boxes and objects wrapped in wash-leather, and five leather bags; by the feel of them containing coin. Not a vast fortune, but a nice competence with the estate, and I was determined that Amelia Lydia should have her share of it; which might not be so easy if he chose to deny the child and then claim his sole legal rights. But I thought I could see a way.

Miss de Bourne, however, still seemed disappointed. "I don't just know what I expected," she murmured. "But it don't look all that much."

"It's worth our trouble and the journey," Pangersbourne replied. "The packages're jewellery. No more than garnets and suchlike, but they'll suit you pretty well. And the bags'll have about two hundred and fifty pounds apiece in 'em. More than enough to fight your case in Virginia and see us comfortable here while I put up this estate for sale."

Dr Caldwell looked at me and I gave a quiet little cough. "Well no, sir," I observed. "It ain't quite so easy."

They both stopped dead, staring in the lamplight, until Pangersbourne demanded, "What the devil do you mean by that?"

"It's a matter of identity. You'll see the difficulty. I think you're Lord Pangersbourne and you say you are. But unless you've got some very certain evidence neither of us can prove it. In such a case the law will require two independent witnesses of good standing. Believe me, sir, our most earnest desire is to assist you all we may," I promised. "And to that end I propose the Reverend Athanasius Hangbolt, who knew you as a boy. And the man Ironband, who was sergeant in your company at Corunna."

You could have heard a pin drop for a minute. And then he exploded again. "I'll be damned if I will." But there was no doubt that the mention of Corunna had frightened him, and once more the lady showed her honesty and good sense; and showed just as clearly that she did not know what had happened there. "For pity's sake where's the harm, Roderick?" she demanded. "If that's what this man and the law require let them have it. Let's have it all clear and straight. And let's get out of this place."

And on that Dr Caldwell had the last word after watching and saying nothing for some time. He announced calmly, "By your leave, sir," and closed and locked the box. "And with your approval, Mr Sturrock, I'll hold the keys," he added. "As a compatriot of this young lady and a close friend of the late Lord Pangersbourne I think I might justly appoint myself referee."

"Nobody could wish for anything better," I assured him. "Shall we go then? We'll call on the parson first."

So we passed out to the stableyard after locking all the doors behind us, and out there the doctor asked softly, "Do I perceive another of your traps, Mr Sturrock?"

I glanced across at Miss de Bourne and Master Roderick, who were now standing a little distance off, waiting for us and talking earnestly together in low tones. "I hope I may be able to spring it," I replied just as quietly. "Otherwise it's a guinea to a pinch of snuff that his lordship will repudiate the child; and then she'll be even worse off than she was before. Will you be good enough to walk ahead with the young lady and engage her in conversation about the Virginia estates and title deeds. I'll follow with his lordship. And you, Jagger, will come on after us. I don't say he'll dare anything reckless, but he might be impulsive, and it's certain that he won't like what I have to say."

My lord seemed just as anxious to talk as I was, and lost no time about it. No sooner had Miss de Bourne and the

170

doctor moved on than he demanded, "Well then, what're you after?"

"It's plain enough," I said. "A provision for the child."

He gave a short laugh. "You're out of your wits. She's nothing to do with me. I never heard of her existence until Smallbrook brought the tale back that she was about the place." I noted the mention of Smallbrook, but did not say anything, and he went on, "You've heard gossip, I suppose? Very well then, if you want the truth, her mother was a whore. She was tumbling with at least one other fellow while she was making a coney of me. I discovered that by chance, and her real name, when I married the bitch. The brat could be anybody's by-blow."

"You may save your breath," I told him. "I know very nearly everything about your marriage. But how much does Miss de Bourne know?"

He laughed again. "As much as you; and very likely more. I made a clean breast of it before we came here. I had to. But she's not one of your vapouring English misses; she's a sensible woman. She understands that a lad of that age can easy make a fool of himself."

"Sensible indeed," I observed drily. "So what's to become of the girl?"

"I don't know nor care. Let her go back to the gutter, where her mother came from. She's got bad blood in her."

"And will Miss de Bourne be sensible about that as well?" He seemed to hesitate then. It looked as if there was already a disagreement on it between them, and I pressed my advantage. "I doubt she will. I fancy she might have more kindness for any unfortunate child. Moreover, I doubt she'll be so sensible about what happened at Corunna either. And I'm very certain she

171

don't know that. Or not yet."

"Corunna?" He stopped so short that Jagger very near blundered into us in the dark. "Corunna?" he repeated, as if he was half strangled. "God blast you, what . . .?"

"What do I know about that also?" I finished kindly for him. "Again pretty near everything. And how do I know? Let's pause a minute while I tell you; it's a matter of simple questions, my lord. We won't go into all of 'em as there are too many and we don't have time. But in brief, why should you be so shy about showing your face in the village in daylight if you were a complete stranger here? And gipsies don't commonly take to strangers, so how could you come to be so friendly with Tickner? And again, why should a stranger be inquiring not after Clara Comfrey's marriage but her death? I suppose one or another of the old actors on Mr Sims' playbill told you about that?"

He did not answer, but it was near enough the mark, and I continued, "You had to find evidence of that to satisfy Miss de Bourne, who is a very proper and respectable lady; and who didn't much like the errand herself. There were several other matters plain enough to a man of my perception, sir. Why should you be searching your late father's study, for one? Because the strong-box was there when you last saw it, in or about 1802, but you did not know that it had been moved to a more secure place two years after you left here, in 1804. So we come to the last question. Why should Roderick Pangersbourne be shy of showing his face in his own village? And there's only one answer to that. In one word, it's 'Corunna'."

He still did not reply, but there was that in his silence which caused Jagger behind us to ask, "Do you want me, guv'nor?" I said, "Not yet," and repeated,

172

"There's only one answer. Ironband was wounded and he was your friend, or he should have been. And you left him and gave yourself up to the French."

"Sir," he demanded between his teeth, "has anybody ever thought of shooting you?"

"Several people," I said. "And they've always bitterly regretted it. Let us finish the tale. You were held prisoner and did not dare apply for an exchange, as was sometimes possible with officers. You'd be released on Bonaparte's first abdication in March 1814; but you chose not to return to England in case either or both Ironband or Clara Comfrey should still be alive. So you found a ship for America. There were plenty of 'em about the French ports at that time."

"Nobody who wasn't there can know what that retreat was like," his lordship muttered, as if half to himself. "Three hundred miles of it, the army in a rabble and damned near starving. Snow and sleet and wolves about us at night Bloody treacherous Spanish guides, and Soult's skirmishers yapping at our heels. And then five blistering years rotting in a French gaol. You've got it right enough, blast you. I found a ship and worked my passage to Boston with a slave-driver of a master. And all for losing my nerve for five minutes. My God, I paid for it."

"Nobody who wasn't there can know what it was like," I mused. "Yet Ironband was, and it'd make an uncommon ugly story if it ever got out. I hope it might not. But let's go on. You made your way to the old American branch of your family, where you were kindly received. Then at some time last year, or early this, they received information of your father's sudden death. This from Dr Birdlip of Wittings End by way of a James Hunter, of Philadelphia; to the effect that the estate here was without claimant. And also offering certain old

173

deeds relating to the Virginian lands in consideration of a debt of five hundred guineas due from the late Lord Pangersbourne. In short the most nonsensical damned wager I ever heard of against some fantastical vegetable. And if I'm any judge of Birdlip," I concluded, "he's refusing to part with your deeds until he sees the money."

I shall not repeat here what he said about Dr Birdlip, but he finished, "And we must have 'em. Patricia has a law suit on her hands concerning the title to the Virginian property. Given those deeds she has a fair hope of winning it. But without 'em she'll lose all."

"Then you're fortunate to have me with you. For I can bring Dr Birdlip to heel any day I choose. If I choose," I added.

"If you choose?" he demanded. "So what d'you want?"

"I've already told you. Full provision for the child, since I doubt you mean to take her back to America with you."

"My God, I don't," he announced. "Very well. We'll say a hundred pounds. And that's generous."

"But not generous enough," I answered sharply. "Come sir, we're near enough at the rectory, and if you want this matter settled without Miss de Bourne learning too much about you it must be settled now. First you will advise her that there is a letter in existence which proves beyond any doubt that Amelia Lydia is your daughter." To confess the truth I did not know whether that letter was still in existence or not, but it sounded well enough, and I continued, "In consideration of which you have agreed to make over the Pangersbourne estate here; this to be held in trust for the child until she comes of age."

"No, by God," he replied, but I continued, "You will

also make over to her one half of the coin deposited in the strong-box. The remainder, and any jewellery or other items, to be retained by yourself. It's not unreasonable."

"It's bloody robbery," he declared. "And worse. I'll see you in hell before I agree to it."

"Then I shall bring the whole case before a judge in chambers," I said. "And you should be warned that the child now has some very powerful friends. You should be further warned that if we have to take it that far the matter of Corunna will appear in the London news sheets. I don't need to tell you what some of 'em might make of that."

There was a silence; and from somewhere ahead Miss de Bourne called impatiently, "What are you doing there, Roderick?" I said, "You've no choice, sir, and very little time," and he cursed me as richly as he had cursed Dr Birdlip. But he was lost, and he knew it, for he demanded, "For God's sake what do I tell her? She'll know I've been forced into an agreement like this."

I knew that I had won then. I answered briskly, "Why, very simple. Explain that I can bring some very serious charges against Dr Birdlip if I choose to. Explain that I can force him to give up your Virginian deeds, and remit any claim he may pretend against the estate. Damn it, sir," I finished warmly, "you're coming out of it very well. You're getting what you came to England to find, and I'm saving you five hundred guineas. You're picking up at least that much again from the strong-box, to say nothing of whatever else may be there, and if I'm any judge that's a sight more than you ever expected. Moreover you may rely on my utmost discretion, and you may be certain that Parson Hangbolt will keep Ironband quiet when he comes out of his liquor. So let's set about the business and have it agreed, with the parson and Dr Caldwell as witnesses."

So that much was settled, though after making all our arrangements it was late when we left the vicarage; Lord Pangersbourne and Miss de Bourne to their own lodgings—wherever those might have been—Dr Caldwell and myself to the inn. Here we discovered that Mrs Oakes had packed Amelia Lydia off to her bed, and Master Maggsy and Jagger off to their stable loft; where they both were no doubt snoring lustily by now. There was little point in further questions or explanations tonight; but I was far from satisfied, for I still could not see any clear way of bringing in the rascal Smallbrook.

"There's the rub," I observed to the doctor as Mrs Oakes served us unwillingly with a damnable slab of cold pie for our supper. "We still have no proof of Pangersbourne's murder. I can frighten Dr Birdlip for his carelessness, and I shall, but the child remains the only one who can give certain evidence. And that's the last thing we can afford."

"Then I'd say forget it," he advised. "You've done pretty well, sir. Take her back to London tomorrow and let it go."

There was no doubt that was the easiest course, although I am not a man to let anything go; but, as it happened, it was the woman Oakes who settled the matter with her ill temper, for she came bustling in to hasten us over our simple meal and chanced to overhear the last. "And amen to that," she said. "I'll say it agen for the last time I hope. The sooner you take yer bliddy selves off from here the better us'll all be pleased."

Neither am I a man to be addressed in such terms as that, and I gave the creature a sharp answer. "It's not

176

our business to please you, mistress," I said. "We shall go when we think fit. We shall remain here for the cricket match, and leave on Sunday." And I cannot but think that it was Providence who prompted me; as He is always ready to prompt the righteous.

Master Maggsy's tale next morning was short and simple. He and the child were barely at the bottom of the steps from the library yesterday, just starting to explore there, when they became aware of others descending after them. Then before the careless wretch had gathered his wits he had found himself seized, hustled into one of the cellars, and the door barred on him. The child being taken likewise recognised Tickner, whom she had no particular reason to fear and who promised ho harm would come to either of them so long as she kept quiet. So with indisputable female logic she had kept exceedingly quiet; but had watched and listened while "the other gentleman" opened the box— saying "There's something here, but we can't take much of it now"—and then gone with them in an utmost appearance of docility. "Though I did leave things for Uncle Sturrock to follow," she assured Maggsy earnestly. "So that I could tell him where to find you. I think that was very clever of me."

I shall omit Master Maggsy's remarks on how long it took us and turn next to Jagger's drunken odyssey. It will be remembered that Ironband had last been seen at an inn just out of Ringwood, The Cricketer's Tavern, and that was where the good fellow started; and he at once discovered some of the curious customs of cricket among these people. For here the blacksmith was well known both for his weakness and for his prowess as the stalwart of the Milton Pangersbourne team; and by dint of his own manner with ostlers—and by proposing that

he meant to lay a heavy wager on the Ringwood side—
Jagger had contrived to extract the whole sorry story.
Simply that Ironband had stopped at The Cricketer's
late on Wednesday and called for mere quart of ale,
which the rascals there laced heavily with gin; making
an obnoxious and dangerous confection known as
Dogsnose.

"Seems that once he starts he can't stop," Jagger
finished. "Slept in the Cricketer's stable Wednesday
night, on the booze afresh Thursday, when they loaded
him into a wagon and brought him on to the Roebuck.
Which the landlord there ain't no friend of Parson
Hangbolt neither, so he fills him up again and carts him
next to the gipsy camp; where I found him dead to the
wide. And likewise found our Peggoty siting there as
calm as custard, and that young lady. Which she says
"You're in no fit state to handle them horses, my man,
and this child can't be allowed to stay here; I'll not be a
party to nothing of this sort, so I'll drive the pair of you
back myself'. Which she done."

"And a pretty tale," I observed. "God only knows
what cricket's coming to."

"You're liable to find out before long," the rude
fellow retorted. "Thanks to you the parson will have it
that I must play for 'em today. Seems to reckon he's
doing me a favour. And God only knows what that
might come to either."

Indeed by now the preparations for the game were well
under way. Several fellows putting stakes and a rope
round the green, two more rolling the pitch, Parson
Hangbolt consulting with three or four others, and
sporting a top hat, pink shirt and white britches; the
Ringwood men just arrived in wagons with a fair crowd
of their supporters all wearing green sashes and favours;

and a right villainous-looking gang. Mrs Oakes setting tables before the inn in the expectation of custom, children scurrying with boxes and benches for the spectators; some of the gipsies congregating, though so far no sign of Tickner or Smallbrook. And Dr Caldwell surveying these further curiosities of English country life with a quizzical amusement.

"A very ancient game," I explained as we took our seats on a bench under the elms. "And not always respectable. It was played even in the thirteenth century here, but the third King Edward denounced it as a mischief which drew men away from their proper archery practice. And King Edward Fourth forbade it on pain of heavy fines, with two years' imprisonment for any gentleman allowing it to be played on his land. It is only as lately as 1784 that the Court of King's Bench ruled that it might be considered a legal sport."

"You must instruct me in its mysteries," the doctor observed. "For I see the ceremonies are about to begin."

The two umpires had now set up the wickets and were conferring with Parson Hangbolt and another gentleman also attired in a top hat—plainly the Ringwood captain—then next tossing a coin. "Deciding the order of play. The captain who wins the toss may elect which side is to bat first. And it looks like the parson," I said, for he was now studying the pitch and looking up at the sky, which was hot but brassy under a threat of rain later on.

"It's a matter of tactics," I continued. "With the ground remaining wet underneath, but starting to dry on top, there might be an advantage in batting first before it begins to break up. On the other hand the parson has to bear in mind the kind of bowlers Ringwood may play, for the right man can make the ball

179

do devilishly odd things in these conditions, and Pangersbourne clearly have the weaker hitting side without Ironband. He might consider it better to put Ringwood in and chance the state of the pitch by the time they're all out. Then he'll know how many runs he has to score; and if he decides his men can't make so many he may order stonewall play to keep 'em out there as long as possible in the hope of it raining again this afternoon and stopping the match; thus making it a drawn game. Contrariwise, however . . ."

"Thank you, sir," Dr Caldwell said hurriedly. "You explain the niceties admirably. I perceive that it's a very serious business."

"This lot might be," Master Maggsy announced, now joining us with Amelia Lydia and overhearing that last remark. "Jagg's got took sporting and swears that if he has to play he means to have a knock and be damned to it. Likewise the tale's got around that Ringwood've nobbled Ironband. And the gipsies're laying two to one against Pangersbourne." He gave Dr Caldwell a wicked grin. "If you ask me it'll finish with a riot before it's done."

And it very likely would if the game went too badly against Pangersbourne, I reflected; for by the look of it most of the gipsies were here now, and more Ringwood supporters arriving by the minute on wagons or horse, lively and cocksure while the Pangersbourne men were just as grim and determined. For the present, however, all seemed peaceful enough; a pretty, rural scene on the village green. A fairish crowd on the boundary by this time; the two Ringwood batsmen walking out to their wickets to the accompaniment of some cheering; Parson Hangbolt taking the ball to open the bowling and disposing his own men about the field, but already somewhat beef-faced.

But I had other matters on my mind and I shall be brief about the Ringwood innings, as there was little of interest save that Jagger started by making a most remarkable catch close by the boundary; thus disposing of one of their best batsmen and winning a roar of approval from the Pangersbourne crowd. Dr Caldwell, however, was watching with little more than polite interest, and when Master Maggsy and the child removed themselves to sit a little way off on the grass we fell to a discussion of the entire affair. "I have had some far more dangerous, and many more important," I said. "But never before have I had a horticultural mystery or poisoning by peppercorns, and all hinging on a mere vegetable."

"Excellently well bowled, sir," I cried, as Parson Hangbolt took out another batsman. But neither shall I dwell too long on our conversation while we watched the match. I have made the better part of the mystery clear enough, except perhaps only the minor matter of Miss de Bourne's watch, and that was very simple. I paused as the parson sent down a wickedly rising ball which damned near took one of the Ringwood batsmen's head off, observed, "There'll be trouble if he does that too often," and then continued, "It was a sentimental possession bequeathed to her by her grandfather, and she was most gratified by its recovery. Nor did she have any notion that Tickner must undoubtedly have dipped it from her pocket. And the rascal still has mine!"

The doctor chuckled softly, somehat somnolent in the sultry heat of the day; now close on one o'clock. But I did not mean to have him fall asleep on either me or the cricket match, and I asked, "And what of your own conversation with Miss de Bourne last night?"

He gave a slow and thoughtful smile. "By what she

181

was telling me if anybody can make a good Virginian out of your new Lord Pangersbourne I guess she will. But she's in more than a mite of trouble herself. Her folk were always Tories, and made no bones about it. And that means they were on the British side in the Revolution. Her grandfather was at Yorktown when your General Cornwallis surrendered to George Washington in '81; which didn't do his health or reputation just so much good. I don't have the hang of the whole story yet, but it seems they lost a good slice of the Rappahannock estate then and more since to some cousin or the other. Her father's been fighting the case on and off for thirty years or more, although a sick man, and Roderick told them about the old Virginia Company deeds when he met up with 'em. Miss de Bourne reckons that given those documents they might have a fair chance of winning at least some of the land back now that feelings have cooled a bit; and I wouldn't be surprised but she's right. She's a considerable determined young woman. And I've offered to use what influence I may."

We gave our attention to the match again as the ninth Ringwood man tried a late cut at another rising ball, just snicked it and got caught by the wicket-keeper. "They'll not stand for long now," I said, but the doctor's mind was still on our case. "A strange business," he mused, "and a very proper achievement, sir; to clear it up to the best satisfaction of all concerned."

"You're too kind, sir," I told him. "But it's not to everybody's best satisfaction. It's not to *my* satisfaction, and that's what counts. So long as I can't touch that rascal Smallbrook, and he remains at large, he'll be a danger to the child one way or another."

On that moment, however, the last Ringwood wicket fell with our Jagger, of all people, making his second

182

remarkable catch in the outfield. "Well I'm damned," said I in wonderment, my voice drowned by the roar from the Pangersbourne men and Maggsy and Amelia Lydia's screeches. "He'll be the hero of the hour. Let us step back to buy him a pot of ale, sir."

We now come to the aforementioned Act of Providence, etc., and the most curious innings of cricket I have ever seen in my life; and notwithstanding my critical publisher I shall allow myself another two or three pages for it. At a little after one o'clock with Pangersbourne yet to bat the position was this: Ringwood all out for one hundred and nine runs, and play to start again sharp at two. The pitch bumpy and getting worse, the heat growing more oppressive, the sky sulphurous and the light blinding. Mrs Oakes doing a roaring trade with several other women helping her, the crowd dispersed all around the boundary, and the gipsies everywhere; but still no appearance of Smallbrook or Tickner.

Parson Hangbolt and the Ringwood captain addressing each other with the utmost courtesy, but otherwise like a pair of fighting cocks in top hats; both consulting their oracles as to tactics. The odds up three to one against Pangersbourne and no takers for a drawn game. Aaron and Moses sitting side by side on the bench outside the inn and croaking like a pair of old ravens. Jagger exhibiting his fearful horse grin, and Master Maggsy and Amelia Lydia now seemingly on the best of terms with a following of village children. Dr Caldwell studying all with quiet interest, as he might have been studying the customs of wild Indians in the forests of the Orinoco; and me with my sure instinct that there was mischief somewhere close by.

Yet there was no open sign of it as Pangersbourne went in to bat. So far as I could see from watching the

183

crowd all attention was on the game and a nice display of both offensive and defensive play; one bat blocking the bowling, and the other hitting out at everything that offered him a chance. This fellow put up some pretty scoring until his partner received a wicked ball in the private parts and fell back on his own wicket with a groan. That incident raised an ugly mutter as he was carried off the field, and drew some surprising remarks from Parson Hangbolt, but he silenced the murmur by commanding, "Quiet, there!" and marching out himself to take his stand. Then the very next ball took his top hat off and such is the fickle nature of crowds that this fetched a burst of laughter. Nevertheless it was poor tactics by Ringwood, for the reverend gentleman's face darkened from beef to beetroot and thereafter he opened his shoulders and hit everything that came his way. Three fours in succession, next ducking to dodge another rising ball whistling past his head, and then a mighty six clean through the window of the inn to a roar from the Pangersbourne men; and a screech of rage from Mrs Oakes.

By three o'clock Pangersbourne were fifty-one for four wickets and seemingly in a strong position, with the parson still keeping up his end, though playing more cautious. But the sky beyond the church was darkening ominously, the heat yet more sweltering, and the entire scene bathed in a horrid yellow glare as if the Devil had opened his furnace doors. Dr Caldwell was dozing gently with his hat over his eyes, Maggsy flat on his back on the grass and snoring—the wretch had never had much interest in cricket—Jagger sitting with the other Pangersbourne batsmen, and the child harmlessly gathering up empty pots for Mrs Oakes. Yet I could still smell mischief.

Where it was I did not know, but so strong was it that

184

I moved away even with the match in the balance—sixty-seven for five with the parson still scoring—and began to work round through the crowd. But there was never a sign of anything untoward except that devilish yellow light and the only sound to be heard was the clock of the bat against the ball. Beyond their wagons on the other side of the green the Ringwood supporters were thick against the rope, and no trees for anybody to lurk behind, only a bit of narrow road and the row of cottages; but not so much as a dog by 'em, and every eye in the field intent on the game. Over by the inn Dr Caldwell and Maggsy now also seemed to be watching, and the child was still plain to be seen with Mrs Oakes.

If the mischief was anywhere it was in those cottages, I thought, though they looked innocent enough, and all of their people out here with their eyes on the game. You could have fired a cannon in the road without causing anybody to turn round to see what it was. The excitement had fallen to a breathless quiet, and I remained long enough myself to see the parson and his partner knock up another eleven before the other man was run out. By this time I had lost note of the score, but a fellow standing close by told me that it was now eighty-seven for seven; "And it'll be a bliddy close thing," he added, not looking a me, but sparing an instant to glance up at the lurid sky.

From here I moved on to the end of the churchyard lane noting for the first time that the last cottage there, behind a little fence, was empty and the windows blank, but when I pushed through the gate to try the front door that was shut fast, though there seemed to be a curious whiff of lamp oil in the air. An empty cottage and a whiff of lamp oil, I thought; yet empty cottages are not all that unusual in the country, and lamp oil is one of the commonest of stinks. There was no sound within, the

185

windows were shuttered inside, and no sign of foot-marks in the dust on the slate doorstep. Neither was there much profit in standing there gazing at the place and I went on to the end of the green, where I could keep an eye on the road and the church lane and watch the crowd at the same time.

The match was now on a knife edge. Another two men gone for only eight more runs; fifteen needed to win and a mutter of thunder in the distance; the parson still there, tired but dogged; the crowd holding its breath as one man; and now Jagger coming out to bat. And the Ringwood bowler plainly intent on a quick end, even if he had to get it by murder, for the first ball he sent down damned near cut Jagger's nose off.

But that was the last of the over and the bowling came back to the parson next. He took two more runs and then tried for another two, but only made one, thus leaving Jagger to face the attack once more; and I doubt if he even saw that ball as it whistled past his head. Over on the other side of the green Master Maggsy screeched into the silence, "You're supposed to hit 'em, Jaggs," and that seemed to annoy him, for hit the next one he did whether he saw it or not; and Jagger was an exceed-ingly powerful young fellow. It went like a cannon shot and I saw the crowd scatter on the boundary; and saw also that Amelia Lydia was no longer there.

"And what now?" I asked, jerking about to the cottages, fifty yards or more away. And, sure enough, there she was. The calamity child herself, skipping gaily along towards the last one. What followed happened quicker than it takes to write. The cottage door was opening, the child at the gate, and I cried, "Peggoty!" But the crowd was roaring its approval of Jagger's stroke and she seemed neither to see nor to hear me. She was looking at somebody in the doorway; somebody she knew but did not realise she had reason to fear. I started to run and to yell again, but on that instant a confounded dog shot out from somewhere clean between my legs and I went down with a mere undignified grunt and a crash which drove all thebreath out of my body.

Dizzied by the fall it took me a minute to get on my knees and by then she was inside the gate and Smallbrook outside the cottage wheedling her to come closer. He was holding out something which shone like gold in one hand; but what I could see, and she could not, was the other behind his back—grasping something with a steely glint in the evil yellow light. And he did not see me either, for he was too intent on her. I tried again to shout, but my voice came out only a breathless croak; while there was another chock of the bat on ball and that damned crowd, which before had been as silent as the grave, must needs then let out another mighty roar.

It was a scene which is imprinted on my eyes for ever; and moments seemed to stretch into eternities as I stumbled on, both cursing and praying. I vowed I would kill that bandy-legged little monster with my bare hands; but there was nothing else I could do. He very nearly had his hand on her shoulder now; and I was too far away, and still reeling from my fall. Nevertheless I shouted again, a cracked yell; and as if in answer that ball came down out of the sky like the Hammer of God.

It took Smallbrook clean between the eyes and he went over like a rag doll. The child gave a little shriek, paused and drew back, staring fearfully at the bloody ruin of his face, and then looking to me as I approached and snarled at her, "What're you doing here?" She replied, "Please, Uncle Sturrock; it was Tickner; he told me Mr Smallbrook would give me your watch if I came to Timbrell's old cottage," and I said, "Get out of

187

this." For the rascal was dead and by no means a pretty sight.

Over on the other side of the green the Pangersbourne men were still cheering, but here the crowd started to stream across the road and press about us and I roared, "Stand back there," above their increasing exclamations and questions as Maggsy came elbowing his way ungently through them. "I wondered where you'd got to," he observed to the child, announced next, "Our Jaggs done it; Jaggs knocked the winning hit," and then stopped very near as still as Smallbrook himself. "God's eyeballs," he whispered. "There's a mess. What done that?"

"Jagger also," I said. "Or an Act of God. You may have your choice."

There is little more to tell. When we came to search the cottage we found kindling liberally soaked with lamp oil, a pony still tethered outside the back door, and the woods beyond Deadman's Mill little more than a hundred yards away across the field. "Devilish," said the doctor, and I agreed. "He could not know that we had discovered the peppermill and laburnum, but he could never be sure that Amelia Lydia wouldn't blab something out. So put her out of the way for safety. Wait for the excitement towards the end of the cricket match to do it, and make his escape to the Forest in the confusion when the fire starts. And he could have done it easy enough. It would have seemed merely another silly child playing with sulphur matches, and nothing ever to attach it to him; or so he imagined in his simple way. It makes my blood run cold."

But that was something else she need never know; so after charging Parson Hangbolt with the formalities of the inquest and leaving a letter for Dr Birdlip—which I

188

calculated would both procure the surrender of the Virginian title deeds and sober him for the rest of his life—we departed in thankfulness for London the next day. There the various arrangements took several weeks to conclude, but all came out well in the end. I kept my promise that the year's rent owing from the village and farms might be conveniently forgotten, and Miss de Bourne and Lord Roderick set sail again for Virginia pretty hopeful. The child was legally acknowledged, agents were appointed to the estate, and she found herself the heiress to some £500, with a further expected yearly income of £400 or so; all to be held in trust for her until she came of age, while my very dear friend Lady Dorothea Hookham-Dashwood kindly consented to superintend her upbringing and education. And finally Dr Caldwell and I parted on the best of terms after a most convivial valedictory supper with Master Maggsy and Jagger, when the good gentleman issued a pressing invitation to visit Philadelphia: an invitation which I am considering with more than a little interest.

We did not catch Tickner, nor did not go far to try, although it was clear that he had loaned Smallbrook my watch to lure Miss Amelia Lydia round to the cottage. In that forest you might as well have tried to catch a weasel on a dark night; besides which I had no wish to tell some country magistrate how Jeremy Sturrock had been knocked over the head and dipped by a little gipsy runt about three-quarters his own size. Some of these rural gentlemen have a bucolic notion of humour. But, for the rest, we parted on excellent terms with Parson Hangbolt, and the most curious *post scriptum* came from him in our correspondence concerning the final matters. The still bloodstained cricket ball, he informed me, is now preserved in a glass case in the taproom of the inn. Known as "Jagger's Ball", it is the centre of

189

attraction for miles around; a source of considerable profit to Mrs Oakes, and the very near permanent lique-faction of the ancient Aaron and Moses in telling the tale of the great Pangersbourne cricket match.

Jeffreys
The Pangersbourne murders